His only chance

Cameron forced himself to lie quietly, something he was good at. Maybe the detectives had known he was awake. Maybe they were trying to bluff. Maybe they didn't know who he was, and they knew they couldn't find out, so they were trying to scare him into falling apart. But if he just stuck to his story, he'd be all right.

And he didn't feel sorry for the Laceys. Where had all the grown-ups been who should have helped him when Pop hurt him? He couldn't tell them—the teachers and coaches—but they must have seen the bruises even though he tried to hide them. The grown-ups should have known—they should have helped him. And what about the parents who should have kept their sons safe, and instead let Hank Miller take them? Cameron didn't owe adults anything. This was his chance, and he was going to take it.

"A highly original novel that is remarkable for its outstanding descriptive narrative and brilliant emotional portrait of a troubled young victim."   —*VOYA*

"Alphin builds the pressure masterfully.... [Her] treatment of each character's psychological wounds is also impressive.... Readers will be enthralled by her suspenseful plot."   —*Publishers Weekly*

OTHER PUFFIN BOOKS YOU MAY ENJOY

Counterfeit Son

ELAINE MARIE ALPHIN

PUFFIN BOOKS

PUFFIN BOOKS
Published by the Penguin Group
Penguin Putnam Books for Young Readers,
345 Hudson Street, New York, New York 10014, U.S.A.
Penguin Books Ltd, 80 Strand, London WC2R ORL, England
Penguin Books Australia Ltd, Ringwood, Victoria, Australia
Penguin Books Canada Ltd, 10 Alcorn Avenue, Toronto, Ontario, Canada M4V 3B2
Penguin Books (N.Z.) Ltd, 182-190 Wairau Road, Auckland 10, New Zealand

Penguin Books Ltd, Registered Offices: Harmondsworth, Middlesex, England

First published in the United States of America by Harcourt, Inc., 2000
Published by Puffin Books,
a division of Penguin Putnam Books for Young Readers, 2002

1 3 5 7 9 10 8 6 4 2

Puffin Books ISBN 0-14-230147-7

Printed in the United States of America

For Art,
who has a rare staying power

Contents

Counterfeit Son

Prologue

He chose the Lacey family at first because of the sailboats. For as long as he could remember he'd dreamed of sailing. He imagined it would feel like flying, the wind rushing past his face and the waves scudding like clouds beneath him. And he thought he would feel safe—no people around, just him and the boat and the open water.

He knew about the sailboats because he'd seen them in the newspaper photographs. He had read everything about the boys, all the clipped articles on yellowing newsprint, all the magazine features on slick paper so limp it had lost its gloss. Reading about someone else's life was almost as good as dreaming about sailing.

He couldn't remember exactly when he had discovered the file cabinet in the corner of the small cellar storage room. Pop always locked him in the cellar while it happened. He hated the cellar—he hated the blows and the cries from upstairs, muffled only slightly by the locked door and the flooring, and he hated the smell. Pop kept spreading quicklime and fresh earth over the dirt floor, but the smell never went away completely. You could hardly smell anything upstairs, but when he was shut down in the cellar the thick, sickly sweet odor got inside his nose and he couldn't get rid of it. If he breathed through his mouth, he tasted it—a heavy taste like a rabbit a dog had torn apart and left half-buried in rotting leaves.

He remembered that he had been trying to blot out the smell when he first stumbled onto the file cabinet. If he closed himself in that little side room, the odor wasn't as bad. He had shut the door and pulled a dangling chain, and a single lightbulb flicked on overhead. There were cardboard boxes piled in the room, sodden from the damp, and he had seen the gleam of metal half-hidden behind them. The file cabinet was up on two-by-fours, and if he slipped around the shadowy side of the boxes he could open the drawers easily. The clippings were inside.

He wasn't the greatest reader. He couldn't remember much about starting school, but he knew he'd been kept back. One of the boys had tried to help him with his reading once, and he'd gotten better, but he didn't like to think about that. That boy was in the cellar now, with the others, and he didn't have to think about him anymore. He could think about sailing instead.

In school his classmates were always younger, and the teachers never bothered about him. He stayed quiet and kept to himself and didn't learn much, but Pop said that didn't matter. What mattered was not getting noticed. Other kids were problems and took all the teachers' attention. Grown-ups didn't waste any efforts on a kid who kept his mouth shut and stayed out of trouble and passed, even with Cs. So when he first looked through the files he had trouble reading the articles. He recognized some of the pictures, though, from the boys he remembered, and he started with the articles in those files, sounding out the letters until the words made sense.

His reading improved, and over the years he read every article in the file cabinet. Some he read over and over. He knew each boy's family as if it were his own, and he chose the Laceys because of the sailboats. He also chose them because the boy's looks and age were close to his own, and because they had moved into their house only six months before their son disappeared. That would help explain his not knowing his way around.

And he also chose the Laceys, in the end, because of their money.

1

Return from the Dead

"What?" The officer ran a hand through his un-combed hair and bent down across the high counter in the Buckeye police station lobby. "Say that again."

Cameron Miller swallowed and forced himself not to back away. If he couldn't make himself go through with it now, he might as well give the whole thing up.

"I'm Neil Lacey," he whispered. "I got away. I need help."

People rushed past the policeman, phones rang, and from the look of his rumpled uniform and his bristling jowls, the officer staring at him must have been up for a couple of nights straight. This was the only police station in Buckeye, and Cameron thought they'd probably been taking the heat on Hank Miller's shooting.

"Kid says he's Neil Lacey," he heard the officer at the counter tell another officer. Cameron swallowed again and made himself look steadily at the two of them. It wasn't easy, after years of ducking his head so no one could look him in the eye.

"But—" The second officer pressed his lips together and didn't finish.

"I know." The rumpled officer looked perplexed. "What do we do with him?"

The second officer shrugged. "I'll take him into B. You call Simmons." He beckoned. "Come on, uh, Neil."

Cameron followed the officer down the hall, his knees weak and trembling. *Don't tell the cops anything,* Pop had told him the time police officers came to question them about Cougar. *If you do, they'll see just how bad you are. They'll take you away and lock you up, and you'll find out what punishment really is.* He'd known he was bad, so he'd done what Pop said. He'd acted the part, like he did at school, and the cops had gone away. So had Cougar.

Now, after trying so hard to obey Pop's rules for as long as he could remember, Cameron had broken this rule, blown it to bits, and he was terrified of the consequences. But what other choice did he have?

The officer led him into a room with a metal table and four folding chairs. "Sit down, uh, Neil. Look, can I get you anything? A Coke, maybe? Or a sandwich?"

Cameron wondered what he should do. What would ring true? "Could I have a Coke, please?" he asked. Then, on an impulse, he added, "When can my parents get here? I really want my dad."

The officer twisted his gold wedding ring. "I don't

know—I'm sure they'll be here soon. I'll get you that Coke." And he fled the room.

The walls were blank except for a chalky gray-green coating of paint. The room didn't have any windows, just like the cellar storage room. There weren't any boxes or file cabinets, but Cameron didn't need to look in the files. He had learned everything they could teach him.

He looked at the door. It was probably locked, but he was used to being locked into rooms, and this one was okay. There was plenty of light, and it smelled of a mixture of fresh pine cleaner and stale cigarette smoke—safe smells. And, in spite of the fear, he didn't hurt as much as he usually did. His left arm and side still ached from the last beating, but the worst of the pain had worn off. Pop had been excited about looking for a boy again, after so long, and had left him in the house alone for a few nights before ... before the shooting. Cameron felt a strange ache in his chest, and he wished he could run home and find Pop waiting for him. He'd confess what he'd done and take his punishment gladly, if only Pop could still be there to look after him. Now he had to look after himself, and he didn't know if he was strong enough.

Cameron laid both hands flat on the tabletop and stared straight ahead. He'd had plenty of practice in shutting out his surroundings and his fears. In his mind, he sailed across deep blue water shimmering with flecks of gold. The wind blew fresh against his cheeks, spattering his eyelashes with a fine spray.

The door banged open and he jumped. There were three men now: the officer, who placed a can of Coke on the table, and two men in suits.

"Here's your Coke, son," the officer said. "This is Detective Simmons and Special Investigator Colbert."

Cameron stared at the two men and wrapped his hands around the cold can. "Are my parents coming?" he asked.

The men looked at each other. "In a little while," Detective Simmons said, sitting down facing him. "Now, Neil—why don't you tell us what happened? You told Officer Norton you got away. How did you do that?"

He placed a small black tape recorder on the table.

Cameron licked his lips and eyed the tape recorder, listening to its soft hum. "He put me down in the cellar—" he started.

"He—who?" the detective asked quickly.

"Hank Miller. He always put me down in the cellar." The words came, painful but convincing, because they were the truth. "He'd lock the cellar door until it was over." Cameron swallowed some of his Coke and stared at the recorder. Knowing what to say was easy—saying the words aloud was hard. *They'll know,* he heard Pop's voice. *They'll know how bad you are.* His stomach cramped from the cold drink.

He made himself go on. "He hadn't had anybody in a while, so I hadn't been down there in a long time. But then he brought home Josh." He saw the two men in suits look quickly at each other.

"That night, he locked me in the cellar. I tried to

warn Josh." Cameron felt tears sting his eyes, surprising himself. "I told him to do what"—he caught himself before he said *Pop*. Neil wouldn't think of Hank Miller as Pop. He went on, hoping they hadn't noticed— "Hank said, but he didn't listen. None of them listened." He gripped the can tightly to stop the words. He didn't want to talk about the other boys.

"When Hank was finished he unlocked the door. He was real nervous, though, and angry. He made me help him dig another hole in the cellar floor—it's all packed dirt down there, hard to dig deep, but just dirt."

Words—how could they show these men in their pressed suits what it was like to stand on the shovel, using your weight to make it bite deep, then pull back on it with all your strength to lever the dirt out, all the while panting with the effort and choking on that smell?

He didn't try. "It was morning by the time we finished, and I asked him if I should go to school. He said yes, he didn't want to attract any notice by messing up the routine. He was real big on routine. But I thought I'd get in trouble because I was so tired, and anyway, it was the last week of school so I didn't think the teacher would tell him I'd cut. So I left like I was going to school, but then I went in the woods behind the house and I hid there to go to sleep."

The special investigator hadn't said anything yet, but Detective Simmons nodded. Cameron thought the cops were probably almost as familiar with that patch of eastern Tennessee woods as he was. When they'd closed in on the house, some of the officers had come through the trees.

"I woke up when I heard people moving in the woods," he went on. "I got my book bag and stayed out of sight, and I heard them come up to the house. I heard talking and then shouting. I don't know what happened next, but then I heard gunfire and more shouts." He knew what had happened, all right, but he didn't think Neil would have cared enough about Hank Miller to figure it out. *Pop must have fought back,* Cameron thought. He knew Pop had a gun, though he'd never shot any of the boys, of course. *He must have shot at the police, and they shot back.*

Cameron turned the can around in his hands and stared at the shiny red metal. Then the distorted reflection of his face in the slick redness made him feel sick, and he put down. "So I ran away."

"Why did you run?" the detective asked him.

Cameron shrugged. "I was scared. I was afraid Hank was in trouble because of Josh, or the others. I was afraid I'd get in trouble, too."

The two men glanced at each other again. "What did you do then?"

"I hid out that night. Then, in the morning, I went back to see if things were okay. But there were cops all over the place, and those yellow streamer things circling the house. I didn't know what to do, so I listened for a while." He swallowed, remembering how his brief surge of relief had quickly been replaced by fear, and by a loneliness so intense it had shocked him. "That's when I heard Hank was dead."

"So you came here," Detective Simmons said, leaning back in his chair.

Cameron shook his head. "Not right away. I was scared. I thought about it for a while first. I mean—I'm fourteen. I thought maybe I could get home to Freeport on my own, but I was afraid to try."

The detective stared hard at him, his eyes narrowed. *He doesn't think much of me,* Cameron realized, flushing helplessly. *He thinks I'm a major wimp. Well, I guess I am.*

After a few moments Detective Simmons nodded, and the rumpled officer brought in another man, a young officer in a crisp uniform. This man looked like he'd gotten some sleep, not like the others. He must not have been in on the raid.

"Do you recognize this man?" the detective asked.

Cameron stared harder at the officer. He did look familiar.... Then Cameron started. "I—yes, I do."

"When did you see him before?"

"He—he came to the house," he stuttered, remembering the young officer and his questions about Cougar, who had once been Pop's friend. Cameron felt as though he were going to throw up the Coke he'd drunk. "He asked me questions."

"Why didn't you tell the officer who you were then?" the detective asked, his voice hard. "Why did you say you were Hank Miller's son, Cameron?"

"He—Hank always said to say that—he told everybody I was his son—he said not to say anything to the cops—he told me they'd lock me up and punish me—he said he'd kill me—"

"Why did he keep you alive?" Detective Simmons demanded. "He killed over twenty boys—why were you special?"

"Ease up," Investigator Colbert said, but no one paid any attention to him.

"Because I did what he said," Cameron whispered. He wanted to tell them he'd bought the right to stay alive, bought it with nights of white-hot pain and days of aspirin-choked silence. He'd paid the price because he'd dreamed that someday Pop would finally tell him he was good, and the nightmare would stop. But he couldn't say that to these men. They'd see how bad he was and know he was lying, and he'd never get his chance to sail free.

The angry face swam in front of his eyes. "Are you Cameron Miller?" Detective Simmons asked.

Cameron pushed his chair back from the table and stood up unsteadily. The room spun around him.

"I'm Neil Lacey," he said, through lips that felt numb and swollen, as though Pop's fist had smashed his mouth. He slid into blackness as the table edge slipped away from his fingers and the floor rushed up to meet him.

2

Positive I.D.

In the dream, he lay on a hard bed in a darkened room. *You've been bad,* the man told him. *Now be good, and everything will be all right.* The man lay down beside him and drew a single sheet over the two of them. *Don't cry,* the man said. *Don't make a sound.*

He lay on his side and felt the man pressing close to his back, strangely comforting but also threatening. He willed himself not to shudder as the man reached one arm around to hold him and turn him face down on the mattress.

Don't cry, the man repeated, his voice low and his breath coming in hot jabs against his ear. *Don't struggle. Be good.* And he lay still, wide-eyed in the dark, the wrinkled sheet dry beneath his face, his teeth clenched, and he let the man do what he wanted.

Cameron made himself wake up when he felt the

damp pillow under his cheek. Pop would beat him, he thought wildly, or worse—the cellar! He never cried—

Then he remembered that Pop was dead. Cameron lay there rigidly in the strange bed, his eyes closed, the damp pillowcase pressed against his face. The empty space inside him that Pop had left seemed to swell like a balloon, pressing against his lungs until he could barely breathe. He wished he could slip back into the familiar dream, and he wished he could forget it forever. Suddenly he realized he could hear voices, and he strained against the ache in his chest to make out what they were saying.

"I think we'd better call his parents right away."

"Are you sure they *are* his parents?" Cameron recognized the hard voice. That was Detective Simmons.

"Everything he said rang true," the first voice said.

"And the scarring and other physical damage is consistent with his having endured six years with Miller," a different voice added. "He's got eleven different bones that were broken and left to heal badly. He's suffering from—"

"Why only six years?" Simmons interrupted. "Why not his whole life? He said he was Cameron Miller before. Maybe he *is* Miller's son."

"Then why say he's Neil Lacey?" the first voice asked.

Someone, probably Detective Simmons, snorted. "Obviously he wants a fancy home, well-off parents. Look, Colbert, you're new to this business. I've seen too many hysterical parents and too many unhappy endings.

If this were a fairy tale the kid would be Neil Lacey, but this is real life."

There was a heavy thud, as though a meaty fist had slammed into a wall or something. "These serial killers make me sick!" Simmons went on, his voice thick with disgust. "Miller was a monster who tortured kids, and that boy went along with it. Now he doesn't want to be charged with being an accessory."

The detective's harsh voice seemed to pulse with a controlled fury. Cameron shuddered inside. The tone sounded like Pop's when he was explaining why he was about to use the belt. "Look, Colbert, we're talking about a crime here. What Miller did—that had nothing to do with sex or love. We're talking kids—the youngest was just seven. It's not love at that age—it's not a gay man who's trying to find someone to love—it's a man who hates and despises and uses someone who's weaker than he is! That's why they call it abuse—it's about being in control, it's sadistic violence, it's torture, and it's criminal! And this kid was part of it. Even if he gets off juvenile detention, he'll be stuck in the child welfare system and given potluck with foster parents."

Cameron winced and forced himself to lie motionless. The sheets were smooth and smelled like the fresh air in the woods behind Pop's house. He couldn't remember sleeping on smooth, cool sheets like these.

"Whoever he is, he's a victim, not a criminal," the first voice, Colbert's, said mildly.

"He stood by and let Miller kill over twenty kids!" Detective Simmons said, his voice barely below a shout. "Don't tell me he didn't know what was going on—he probably even participated in the torture! He could have told someone, a teacher at school, a cop—but he didn't."

The hate in Simmons's voice swept over Cameron. The aching emptiness in his chest was dwarfed by the weight of his guilt over the boys, and that weight seemed to press him into the clean hospital sheets. It was no different from Pop's weight crushing him into the sagging mattress back home. He wanted to scream out, *It was Pop who hurt them, not me! I was in the cellar—I never hurt one of them.*

But Cameron knew he was guilty anyway. He couldn't have told anyone, not told and survived, but he should have tried harder to make the boys be good. If they had only listened to him... He dimly remembered one boy who had tried to do what he said. The boy had been obedient and let Pop do what he wanted, and he'd stayed with them for more than three weeks. Cameron had thought he'd have a brother, and things might not be so hard. But then the boy cracked. He began screaming and throwing things, and Pop shoved Cameron into the cellar, where he squeezed himself into the far corner of the little room and covered his ears and still felt deafened by the boy's cries. How could he ever explain that to Detective Simmons?

"He was afraid," Colbert was saying. "He was tortured, himself, from the day Miller kidnapped him. Those scars—"

"Those scars are something else," Simmons said. "They date back six years, right, Dr. Oshida? Well, why not seven? Can you positively say that those early scars couldn't date back seven years, to before Neil Lacey disappeared?"

"Of course not," said the other voice. So he must be a doctor. "There's no way to be sure."

"I'm sorry, Simmons, but you've got nothing to prove he's Cameron Miller," Colbert said. "Personally, I think he's Neil Lacey. He looks exactly like the latest computer-enhanced projection of what the Lacey boy should look like at this age."

Cameron nearly sighed aloud in relief. He'd thought from the photographs in the magazines and newspapers that he was a good match, and now he was sure. How could they argue with a photograph?

"Brown hair, hazel eyes, short, and skinny?" the detective scoffed. "Couldn't be more ordinary. Am I right, Dr. Oshida?"

"Ordinary, yes," the doctor said. "But his facial features are consistent with the Lacey features."

"Look," Colbert said urgently, "if we hold him and don't inform his parents, his father could slap us with a lawsuit so quickly—"

"To help Cameron Miller?"

"To make us release Neil Lacey."

"I say we don't trust those happily-ever-after maybes you'd like to believe in," Simmons insisted. "Wait for positive identification."

Cameron lay rigid. How could they identify him positively?

"If we wait," Colbert said coldly, "and the hospital prints match, his father is going to break you to a beat. And I'm not going with you."

"Fine! Okay! Call them," Simmons told him. "Tell them their son is back from the dead. They'll believe it because they'll *want* to believe it. Then when the prints come back and say he's not their boy, you take the rap. Because then the father sure as hell *is* going to sue!"

There was a pause, and Cameron's thoughts raced. He hadn't figured on prints. Why would anybody print a little kid?

"How long will it take to hear from the hospital?" Colbert asked.

"It will be quicker if we inform the parents," the doctor said. "I explained that from the beginning. You can't very well send a routine inquiry to every hospital in Knoxville asking if Neil Lacey was born there and would they fax his toeprints to us. If the mother tells us what hospital he was born in, and authorizes the inquiry, we can have the data within twenty-four hours."

"This is a serial killer investigation—" Simmons started.

"This is a child," the doctor said. "Whoever he is, he's not your serial killer. You've already taken care of Hank Miller."

The voices were silent for a few heartbeats. Then Colbert said, "I'm going to call his father."

There was a loud crash, as though a door had been jerked open violently and slammed against a wall. "You do what you want," Simmons said, and his footsteps faded into the distance.

"Is he awake?" Colbert asked after a moment.

"I doubt it," the doctor said. "I gave him a sedative, and he should still be out. Who do you think he is?"

"I think he's Neil Lacey," the special investigator said flatly. "He's got to be. How in the world could he get away with walking into a strange family and pretending to be their long-lost son? He'd be caught the first time they expected him to know something and he drew a blank."

"Not necessarily," the doctor said. "Complete or partial amnesia is perfectly consistent with the sort of trauma this boy has lived with. Considering his age at his abduction, he may well have only the vaguest memories of his life before Hank Miller took him. His family isn't going to get back the eight-year-old they lost, you know."

Amnesia, Cameron thought, feeling strangely relieved. That would explain a lot—not only how he could deal with the Laceys, but a lot about himself, too. He'd never had a very good memory. Other kids at school remembered all sorts of weird things—birthday parties when they were four or five, how they fell off their two-wheeler learning to ride it without training wheels, the first time they camped out or went fishing.

Of course, he'd never done any of those things, or at least didn't think he had. Cameron definitely didn't have any memories of that sort of specific moment in his life, and that bothered him sometimes. He especially didn't like the fact that he couldn't remember his mother. But the doctor said people could tell what Pop had done to him by the marks on his body. And he said that the beatings, and the other things, could cause amnesia. Maybe it was because of Pop that Cameron couldn't remember things like other kids could.

"You mean," Colbert said slowly, "all he has to do is say he can't remember anything he used to know?"

"Well, I'm sure he'll find memories resurfacing," the doctor said. "His family will certainly try to stimulate his memory. What I'm saying is that if someone wanted to pretend to be Neil Lacey, and if he had enough nerve, he could probably pull it off."

"*Could* he be Cameron Miller?" the special investigator asked.

"Right now he could be anybody," the doctor said. "But not for long. As soon as we look at those toeprints from the hospital we'll know for sure. If you have a gut feeling, I'd advise calling the parents now."

The door opened again, and closed. Cameron listened to the silence for a while, then cautiously opened his eyes. He was lying on a hospital bed with metal railings on the side. They didn't make him feel caged. The railings made him feel curiously safe.

There was a second bed in the room. A boy lay on it with tubes hooked up to his arms and his nose. He seemed to be unconscious.

They had thought Cameron was sleeping, too. He was glad of that. But what could he do about these toeprints? He hadn't realized anybody would take prints of a kid. What would they do with him after they compared the prints? Lock him up, like Simmons had threatened? *Punish you,* Pop's words whispered in his memory, *because you've been so bad.*

Cameron forced himself to lie quietly, something he was good at. Maybe they had known he was awake. Maybe they were trying to bluff. Maybe they didn't know who he was, and they knew they couldn't find out, so they were trying to scare him into falling apart. But if he just stuck to his story he'd be all right.

At least they were going to call Neil's parents. The cops had said his father was a lawyer, and Cameron remembered that from the newspaper articles. Detective Simmons said the parents would want to believe in him. Once the Laceys got there, they'd protect him. He felt a wrench of guilt at the lie he was handing them. Could he really use the Laceys like this after they'd lost their own boy?

Then he stopped feeling sorry for them. Where had all the grown-ups been who should have helped him when Pop hurt him? He couldn't tell them—the teachers and coaches—but they must have seen the bruises even though he tried to hide them. The grown-ups should have known—they should have helped him. And what about the parents who should have kept their sons safe, and instead let Hank Miller take them? Cameron didn't owe adults anything. This was his chance, and he was going to take it.

Cameron closed his eyes again. The sheets were so smooth and comforting, tucked around him. He rolled over, away from the damp patch on his pillow. *It's okay to cry,* he told himself, *but you don't have to lie in it.*

3

Pet Names

New voices woke him. Wary, he lay motionless again, trying to figure out what was going on.

"Neil?"

It was a woman's voice, tense, afraid, but hopeful, too. Cameron felt the world spin crazily around him, as though the bed rested on a giant Tilt-a-Whirl, like the ride at the school carnival. What had happened with the prints?

"Son?" This voice was cautious. It was the voice of a man who might ask questions and listen to the answers before administering punishment.

"I gave him a sedative," the doctor told them, "but it should have worn off by now. Come on, Neil, wake up."

Cameron felt a hand fall unexpectedly on his shoulder, and he jerked away, his eyes flying open.

The doctor stepped back, looking alarmed. Then he

said, "I'm Dr. Oshida, Neil. Do you know who these people are?"

Cameron blinked his eyes, shivering. The sheet had fallen away, and he was wearing some twisted wrap-around garment that barely covered him. He saw Investigator Colbert standing behind the doctor and pulled the sheet up. Then he looked at the two people standing beside the bed, and he caught his breath.

The woman had long golden hair swept back neatly into a knot at the nape of her neck. She had deep brown eyes, and she was trying to smile at him, although her lower lip was trembling and her eyes were wide and glittering with unshed tears. But the man—he had Cameron's own long nose, and his too-big ears. And he had the same hazel eyes. Cameron couldn't believe it.

"Dad?" he tried to say, and the word came out a croak. *Not "Pop,"* he thought, *not "Pop" ever again.*

"Yes," the man said, blinking his eyes rapidly. "Neil— oh, Neil. We'd nearly—" He broke off abruptly.

Cameron turned to the woman. She was crying now, silently, tears slipping down her cheeks as she tried to smile.

"Mom?"

"Baby—" And suddenly her arms were around him, enfolding him, smothering him. He went rigid with shock, his brain screaming at the memory of strong arms crushing him against another body. But this embrace was different—he shut his mind to the other vision and leaned against her, breathing the soft flower scent of her hair.

"When can we take him home, Dr. Oshida?" the man asked. "Tonight?"

"No," Dr. Oshida said firmly. "I need to complete some tests before we can release him, Mr. Lacey, and some of the labs aren't open over the weekend. You or your wife will be welcome to stay with him, of course, but I can't let him go home before sometime on Monday, at the earliest."

"I'll stay," the woman was saying. "I can stay through the rest of the weekend, and I'll call the museum and tell them I won't be in the first part of the week. Glenn can take over for a few days—he's always wanted the curator job, anyway."

Cameron wondered who would stay with Neil's brother and sister. Their father? Their mother didn't seem worried about them. He supposed she was just so relieved to get Neil back, she wasn't thinking about the kids who hadn't disappeared.

"What tests?" Mr. Lacey asked, his voice expressionless.

Dr. Oshida lowered his voice. "We've taken complete X rays, but we also need to run a CAT scan and a battery of psychological tests—"

"Oh, but—" The woman released Cameron and sat on the side of his bed, one arm around his shoulders. He felt confused and frightened. Could those tests prove that he wasn't Neil?

"No." The man's voice was flat.

"But, Mr. Lacey—" the doctor began.

Investigator Colbert spoke for the first time. "This is part of an official investigation, Mr. Lacey."

"I understand that. Dr. Oshida may run any tests the police and your task force require to check Neil's physical condition," the man said. "But his family will be the judge of what psychological examinations he needs."

The doctor and the investigator glanced at each other. Then Dr. Oshida said, "Mr. Lacey, I explained that this trauma may have caused amnesia and other psychological problems—"

"I understand," the man said. "I appreciate your concern, Dr. Oshida. But Neil is coming home with us as soon as the last physical tests are complete. We will arrange for private counseling as soon as he has settled in, and it will be with a therapist who is not answerable to the police. As long as Neil stays in the hospital, my wife or I will remain with him at all times, and if you attempt to order any unnecessary examinations or cause any delays, I will apply for a habeas corpus to immediately remove my son from this facility. Do we understand each other?"

Investigator Colbert nodded. "Perfectly."

Dr. Oshida said stiffly, "We will require the dental records to confirm your identification."

"Of course. We'll have the children's dentist fax them to you Monday morning. Feel free to give Neil a full dental examination before he leaves so you can be sure of the match."

Cameron wondered what had happened to the toe-prints, whatever they were, but the man—his *father*, he reminded himself—was staring at him. "Personally, I'm already convinced," he told the doctor.

Dr. Oshida looked back and forth from him to the

man. "Yes," he said, smiling gently. "I can understand why. It's too bad we couldn't have the maternity ward toeprints to make a positive identification immediately, but as he was born at home—"

"We explained that," the woman—*Mother*—said sharply. "I believe in natural childbirth unless there's something wrong. Neil's birth was perfect."

Dr. Oshida bowed his head. "You were very fortunate, Mrs. Lacey."

"Gentlemen," the man said, "could we have a few minutes alone with our son?"

"Of course," Dr. Oshida said, and he left the room with a polite smile. The investigator followed him, but Cameron saw that he left the door slightly ajar. He was listening from the hallway.

Investigator Colbert didn't believe him, after all. Probably Detective Simmons was there, too, waiting for him to make a mistake.

Cameron looked up at Neil's parents. "I'm sorry," he said quickly, confessing before the accusations could start.

"Neil—" his mother started.

"I'm sorry I went off," he said. "I shouldn't have gone to the video arcade. And I shouldn't have gone with him. I'm sorry."

His father moved quickly toward him, and Cameron barely prevented himself from shuddering when the man reached out and smoothed his hair, then hugged him roughly. But the touch was nothing like Pop's embrace, and Cameron felt his shoulders relax.

"Oh, Neil, we'd nearly given up," his father was

saying, his voice muffled because his mouth was pressed against his hair. Cameron could feel the man's breath blowing jerkily down his neck, and it made him tense up again. "We were afraid you were gone forever," his father said hoarsely.

When he was released, Cameron looked up at them. Why weren't they reminding him how bad he'd been? They were glad to see him now, but punishment was sure to come later. He thought he could take it, but there were so many pitfalls—he still didn't understand exactly about those toeprints, and what about dental records? What would they show? And nobody had said anything yet about the brother and sister he'd read about in the articles—how would they take Neil's return? He was so tired, and the acting had only begun. He'd been good at acting like a normal kid at school, but he didn't have to act with Pop, just obey. Would he be able to sustain a role all the time?

The tears were still sliding down the woman's cheeks. His *mother*, he told himself again—he had to start thinking of her as his mother. He wondered what had happened to the mother he couldn't remember. Had she left because he was too bad, and the amnesia had wiped the memory out? Or maybe she had been bad herself and Pop had punished her, or even killed her. Was she buried with the boys?

Cameron had blanked out so much—deliberate blanks, so he wouldn't make a stupid mistake in school and say something he shouldn't, but also blanks that were an escape. When he was with Pop he'd blank out what was happening, and think of sailing instead. And afterward he'd blank out what Pop had done to him, except for the pain. He couldn't completely escape that, though the bottles of aspirin helped. But how could he have blanked out his mother?

He wondered what it would be like to have a mother now. Mrs. Lacey was still weeping silently, and Cameron wanted to tell her not to cry. What would Neil have said to his mother? Cameron searched his memory of the articles about Neil, the interviews with his parents. He had a sudden image of Neil's mother sitting in a sunlit room, holding a worn picture book about Goldilocks and the Three Bears. Cameron remembered the story. Had Pop told it to him? Probably one of the boys had. There were three bears and a strange golden-haired girl who snuck into their house and took their things, but the little bear caught her in the end. Cameron thought he remembered a newspaper photograph of Mrs. Lacey, because he was sure the caption said that she was pleading for Baby Bear to come home to Mama Bear.

"Don't cry, Mama Bear," he whispered, hoping the words would comfort her.

The effect was electric. Her eyes widened, and her lips parted. The tears disappeared. Cameron was terrified—why had he said that? Had Colbert and Simmons heard? Would they rush into the room and arrest him? How bad would the punishment be this time?

"Neil!" she cried, and threw her arms around him again. Over her shoulder, he saw the man—*Father*, he reminded himself—staring at him in stunned delight.

"You remembered!" she was saying, rocking him in her arms. "You used to call me Mama Bear when you were a toddler and I'd get upset!"

Cameron closed his eyes and sagged against her in relief, letting her rock him. He couldn't believe how lucky he'd been to remember the picture in the clipping. Whatever the doctor's positive identification disclosed now, they would believe he was Neil.

Except, somehow, he hadn't expected the Laceys to be so nice. As the woman held him tightly, Cameron remembered Detective Simmons's accusations, and felt bitterly like Goldilocks, the interloper.

4

Tears

His mother stayed with him Saturday night, although he slept through most of it. Cameron woke in the night and saw her in the light from the hospital corridor. She sat propped awkwardly in an uncomfortable-looking hard chair, her head leaning back, her eyes closed. In her sleep she was still smiling. Both she and the man were beside him all day Sunday, through more tests and poking and prodding. They talked to him, telling him about the house, and about his brother and sister. His mother stayed through the night again, still talking, crying sometimes, and sometimes just smiling at him.

On Monday morning his father came back, this time carrying a small blue nylon duffel bag. He got more X rays taken of his teeth, and Cameron worried about this after what they'd said about dental charts. But the

Laceys didn't seem concerned. They'd made up their minds about him.

Finally, one of the army of nurses took him back to the room where the other boy still lay unconscious. She pushed him in a wheelchair, as though he were too helpless to walk for himself, but Cameron didn't argue. He was exhausted from keeping his balance on the tightrope. His mother walked beside the chair, holding his right hand and still talking. Her voice was getting a little hoarse, but he liked the throaty sound of it.

"Diana and Stevie just can't wait to see you," she was saying. She had said this so often that he couldn't help wondering whether it was actually true. Perhaps they weren't as glad to get a big brother back as their parents were to get a first son. Probably Stevie was ticked off, after being the only boy for so long.

Cameron had read about the smaller children. Stevie probably wouldn't remember Neil too clearly, since he'd just turned three when Neil had been abducted. But Diana had been almost seven—old enough to know Neil pretty well. In the pictures she'd looked sad, and in one newspaper interview she'd said how much she missed her brother and wanted him to come home.

"Stevie started cleaning up his room as soon as that Investigator Colbert called to say you were safe," his mother went on.

Cameron felt sick to his stomach. Apparently Neil was supposed to share a room with Stevie. If the younger boy had had the room to himself all these years, he would probably be mad at having to start sharing it again. Not the best way to make friends with the kid.

And Cameron was nervous about sleeping in the same room with somebody. He was used to sleeping alone, except when Pop was there. He could remember waking suddenly in the dark to the sound of Pop's breathing, and knowing what was about to happen. Could he ever sleep with another person breathing so close to him? Also, he dreamed a lot. He'd had plenty of practice in keeping his dreams quiet, but what if the kid noticed anyway? He wished he could ask for a room alone, but he guessed instinctively that Neil's parents wanted to pretend everything was just the way it had been before. If Neil had shared a room with Stevie six years ago, then he would have to share one now.

His father looked up as they came into the hospital room. "I've got you all checked out, Neil," he said, and picked up the blue nylon bag and tossed it gently at him, grinning broadly. "Don't want to go home in your designer gown, I guess."

Cameron smiled back and unzipped the bag. Inside he found new underwear, still in the plastic wrap, and white socks with the paper band still around them. There was a stiff new pair of jeans, and a new Dallas Cowboys T-shirt. He looked at it a moment before remembering they were a football team. Had Neil been a big football fan? Pop mostly watched wrestling, and so Cameron stared at the TV with him, but he didn't like it much.

His mother went out while he dressed, fumbling a little with the new clothes, and with the effort of keeping his back turned away from his father without being obvious about it. The last thing in the bag was a pair of green-and-white running shoes, so new that fresh rubber and leather smells filled the bag. *Expensive, like the other stuff,* Cameron thought. He'd been right about the money. He wasn't greedy, but he still thought he'd be safer if the family had money.

He finished tying the laces and looked up. "Thanks," he said, meaning it. "Dad," he added quickly.

His father blinked his eyes rapidly. "Oh, Neil," he said huskily. "A few clothes—it should have been years of clothes—" He turned away, interrupting himself.

"Dad . . ." Cameron started.

"Neil—I've got to say this—you've got to know—" He broke off again and stood, leaning against the wall with his fists pressing against the clean white paint, the tendons stiff and knotted beneath the sleeves of his striped golf shirt. "That man—what he did to you—"

Cameron's hand clenched on the handle of the blue nylon bag as his stomach lurched. He'd been stupid to try to hide his back. Of course they knew—about the scars, and about the rest. The doctor had said he could see what had happened. For all Cameron knew, they could figure out from the bodies of the other boys what had happened to them, too. Pop always told him not to tell. *They'll know you've been bad,* Pop's memory reminded him. This man, his father now, was going to punish him, just as Pop had said.

"I'm so sorry—" his father was saying, his voice thin and strained. "I wish the police hadn't killed him. I'm so furious I want to take him in my own hands and kill him myself for what he did to you. Neil—" His father suddenly turned and gripped his arms, and Cameron was shocked to see tears running silently down his cheeks. He hadn't realized the man was crying. He couldn't hear it in his voice.

"Whatever he said to you, Neil, don't believe it. It wasn't your fault. He was an animal, Neil, and you survived, and I'm so proud of you, son."

Cameron stared into the hazel eyes that mirrored his own so uncannily and realized that this man wasn't blaming him. He wasn't going to punish him. Pop had lied.

Something cracked inside of him. His eyes blurred, and Cameron felt salty warmth on his cheeks and discovered that he was crying. He caught his breath, and then knew it was all right. If Neil's father was crying, it must be all right for Cameron to cry, too.

His father loosened his grip on his arms and pulled him close in a rough embrace. Cameron should have been frightened by being held so close, but all he could do was cry. He couldn't remember ever crying like this. He had even been afraid to cry down in the cellar, in case Pop came looking for him before he was finished with the other boy. He'd done that a few times. Cameron cried once in a while in a corner of the school yard, but he didn't dare cry much. He was afraid Pop would find out. *All those years of held-back tears,* he thought. *That's a lot to make up.*

"What's this?" It was his mother, and he could hear she was frightened. His father hugged him tightly, then released him and gave him a watery smile. "Just a man-to-man talk," he said, wiping his eyes without any sign of embarrassment.

Cameron ducked his own head and grabbed a corner of the sheet from his bed to scrub his own eyes with.

"Neil, are you all right?" his mother asked, still worried.

"Yeah," he said, surprised to hear how strong his voice was. "I'm fine, Mama Bear."

And she laughed at that, so he guessed she wasn't frightened anymore.

"Come on, then," she said. "We're going home."

He followed them down the hospital corridor, on foot for the first time instead of in a wheelchair. Double glass doors fell open in front of him with a gentle *whoosh* of air, and then he was outside, under a clear blue sky, hearing the rush of engines and spinning of tires.

"They let me pull the car around to here," his mother said, and Cameron followed them to a new Lincoln Town Car, sleek and dark blue. He was certain it couldn't be six years old, and he felt relieved at not having to recognize it.

His father held the passenger door open for him. "You sit in the front seat," he said, his voice light and full of happiness. "I'll get in the back and try to close my eyes while your mother drives."

"You'll do no such thing," she said, laughing. "You go ahead and drive, Jon."

"I'll sit in the middle," Cameron suddenly volunteered. "You can drive, Dad. And Mom, you can sit on the other side."

His father cocked his head to one side. "It'll be crowded."

Cameron smiled. "I don't mind."

Cameron slid over the soft blue plush of the seat and sat in the uneven space in the middle. He was a little scared at being sandwiched in between two people, but at the same time it felt strangely safe, like the metal railings around the hospital bed. He leaned against his mother to give his father room to work the gearshift, and felt suddenly tired.

As the car backed smoothly out of the parking space and swung around, Cameron caught sight of a police car on the side of the ambulance parking area. He flinched at the sight.

"Neil, are you all right?" his mother asked.

"I'm sorry," he said automatically. "I'm okay."

He was glad he'd sat securely wedged between them. The driver's window of the police car was rolled down, and through the Lincoln's windshield he could see the face of the detective who had questioned him so closely—Detective Simmons, the man who didn't believe he was Neil Lacey.

5

Homecoming

Cameron wasn't sure what he'd expected. The pictures of the sailboats in the file had just shown a wide green lawn with a few trees, a small redwood dock, and the boats. He hadn't really thought much about the house itself.

It wasn't a mansion, Cameron knew that. One of the boys had come from a real mansion, a white house with towering columns, half hidden behind ornate iron gates. He'd seen pictures of that house in a magazine clipping. Cameron remembered the article said that the boy's parents had offered to pay a big ransom. Not that money would have made any difference to Pop.

But this was an expensive house, made of tan fieldstone that gleamed golden in the late-afternoon sun, with a curving drive that ran up to a stone entryway. There was money in this house, like the money in the

Lincoln; enough money to make him feel secure. There were also roses blooming against the fieldstone, and bright pansies lining the entryway. And beside the house, the lawn ran down to a sparkling lake rippling gently in the slanting sunlight.

He'd slept during most of the drive home, giving in to the tiredness and the strain, and blanking out his fear at seeing Detective Simmons. There was heavy traffic getting out of Knoxville during the Monday afternoon rush hour, and his father muttered ·that he was glad he'd driven after all. After a while, Cameron just leaned against his mother and drifted off into dreamless sleep, swaying gently in the smooth, quiet car.

It was the bump as they turned off the main road through Freeport onto the lakefront road that woke him. He sat up apologetically, but when he looked at his mother, it seemed as though she hadn't minded. She had a peaceful look on her face for the first time since he'd seen her.

He watched the houses pass by, with the shimmering lake visible between them. They weren't too close together, not like houses in the city. But they weren't as isolated as his house had been. Pop had built it himself, though Cameron couldn't remember him doing that. Pop had told him he'd deliberately bought that large lot on the edge of the woods. It was far enough from the next lot so that no one could hear Pop when he shouted at the boys—or hear the boys, for that matter. And no one could smell anything strange, even right after he and Pop poured the lime and mercuric acid into the cellar before filling in a new hole. These houses beside the lake were a comfortable distance apart. You had some space, but somebody would hear you if you needed them.

The Laceys' house was at the very end of the lake-front road. For a second Cameron felt a surge of fear, because there were no more homes on the far side of the big stone house. The lake continued past the house to the northwest, but there was nothing on the shore but woods and a plowed field. Then he got hold of himself and saw there was a house next door to the Laceys' on the near side, so it was all right. He made himself look again and saw metal towers supporting power lines running down the field and cutting through the woods, and he guessed that was why there wasn't another house there. It didn't mean anything threatening.

"Look familiar?" his father was asking, his voice a little worried.

"Of course, we've done a lot over the years," his mother said quickly. "We'd just moved in—there wasn't any garden yet."

Cameron nodded. "It looks wonderful," he said, and meant it, and he could feel his father relax beside him.

The garage door swept open suddenly, and his mother opened the passenger door and climbed out, beckoning for him to follow. He was sliding across the seat when he saw two kids come running out beneath the still-rising door and skid to a stop, staring at him. Cameron got out slowly and tried to smile at them.

The girl—his *sister*, he thought—looked a lot like

her mother. She had the same deep brown eyes and golden hair, only hers was sun-bleached paler and cut short, curving around her face. And her face didn't look as friendly as her mother's. Her eyes were narrowed, and as she stared at him she chewed on her lower lip.

The boy was worse. Short and stocky, with thick brown hair and his father's hazel eyes, he slouched behind his sister and glared at Cameron.

"Diana, Stevie, come say hello to your brother," their mother was saying awkwardly.

"Kids," their father said, in a careful voice, "remember what we talked about last night?"

Diana suddenly stopped chewing her lip and walked forward a few steps. Cameron realized that even though he was older, she was a few inches taller than he was. He hoped it wouldn't make anybody suspicious.

"Hi," she said. "Welcome home, and all that."

Her voice was neutral, a lot like her father's. Cameron's throat suddenly constricted. Did Neil have a nickname for his kid sister? She'd expect him to call her that. He tried to remember the clippings, but his mind was suddenly blank. How could he ever have been so stupid as to think this would actually work? Cameron nearly turned and bolted, thinking incoherently that at least he could keep the clothes that way. Or had Detective Simmons followed him from the hospital? Was he just waiting for Cameron to make a mistake? He felt more trapped than he had ever felt in the cellar.

Suddenly Stevie ran right up to him, and Cameron took a step back before he could stop himself.

"Hi, okay? I cleaned out half my stuff, okay? You can have the bed by the window, since you always liked that best, okay?"

"Okay," Cameron said before he knew he was speaking, and he heard their parents laugh.

Stevie frowned at him, then nodded. "Okay, then," he said, and turned and went back inside.

His mother sighed. "He's only eight," she said.

"And he can be a pain," Diana added, smiling at last.

Cameron smiled back at her. "He's probably mad at giving up half his room, too, I'll bet."

She nodded, eyeing him thoughtfully above her smile. "You know how crazy he was about the idea of rooming with you in the new house when he was little. But now he's used to having it to himself."

"Come on inside, Neil," their mother said eagerly, and he saw Diana's smile fade, but she followed them into the garage and on into the house.

The first thing he saw was a big window along the back side of the house, facing the lake. He headed straight for the huge plate-glass window in the living room, leaving his parents behind him, and saw the lake and the boats clearly for the first time. There were two sailboats rocking gently at the dock. One was trim, but big enough for the whole family, and one was a small boat for a single person, its sails neatly furled. On the lawn, up from the lake bank, he saw several pieces of another small boat spread out on the grass. His heart beat wildly at the thought of being close enough to touch his dream.

Diana's voice startled him. "If you'd gotten home early enough we were going to put her together so you could go sailing this afternoon." Her reflection was ghostly in the glass, superimposed on the rustling trees and the glittering lake water. "You never wasted much time in the house. You always wanted to get out on the lake—or has that changed?"

Cameron glanced at her and met her expressionless brown eyes. "I've spent a lot of time cooped up in a house," he said briefly, "most of it dreaming about the lake."

Stevie ran into the living room. "It's too late to go sailing today," he informed Cameron.

"Yeah, I know."

Stevie grinned. "Hey, Neil—if you cross the lake with a leaky sailboat, what do you get?"

The boy looked delighted with himself, and Cameron couldn't help smiling at him. "I don't know," he said. "What do you get?"

Stevie's smile faded. "What do you mean, you don't know?"

Cameron felt himself go cold inside. *Stupid, stupid—to be caught up so easily.* It must have been a riddle Neil liked. He had to pay better attention, to watch out for these things. *Think, think,* he ordered himself. *It's just a little kid's riddle—you can guess it—what do you get if you cross the lake with a leaky—*

He smiled at Stevie suddenly. "Hey, I was only teasing," he said. "What do you get? About halfway across the lake. I can't believe you remembered."

Stevie shrugged. "Dad says it a lot."

Cameron looked back at the lake. How many other family jokes wouldn't he know? How could he ever pull this off? He saw Diana's reflection, studying him. Finally she said, without any enthusiasm, "Well, you can sail halfway across the lake tomorrow."

"I can't wait to get out on it, only—" He broke off, suddenly unsure.

"'Only'?" she prodded.

"When things got bad," he said, "really bad, I used to dream about sailing, about being free, only—it's been so long." His voice cracked without warning, and he swallowed. "What if I can't sail the way I dreamed?"

Diana didn't say anything for a few moments, and he wasn't sure what she was thinking. He realized he hadn't called her anything yet, and wondered if she distrusted him. She hadn't called him Neil, either.

"Don't worry," she told him finally. "It's like riding a bicycle. You never forget."

Cameron stared at the little waves slapping against the dock, wishing he could sit in the small boat and feel it rocking beneath him. He wasn't sure if Diana had meant to comfort him or not. He didn't know how to ride a bicycle, either.

6

Neil's Special Night

"I'm so sorry we didn't get back early enough that you could go sailing today, Neil." Cameron saw his mother's reflection in the glass, closing in on him. It gave him enough warning that he didn't flinch when she placed her hands on his shoulders, uncertainly at first, as if she couldn't believe he was really there. Then her arms slid around his chest and she hugged him from behind. In the window, he saw Diana look down, then move away from them with Stevie.

"We were going to assemble your boat," his father said, coming into the room, "and give you a refresher course so you could get on the water."

Cameron turned, and the hug loosened enough that only one arm rested across his shoulders.

"We'll do it first thing in the morning," the man promised, smiling.

"But it's a weekday," Stevie objected. "You've got to go to the office."

His father ruffled the boy's hair. "Having your brother home is worth taking a few days off, don't you think?"

"I guess," Stevie mumbled. He didn't sound convinced.

"This is a special night," his mother said quickly, "your first night home again, Neil. We want it to be perfect. We thought we'd order pizza."

Diana rolled her eyes. "You always say pizza's not good for us, Mom."

Mrs. Lacey glanced quickly at her, then hugged Cameron's shoulders again. "Yes, but this is a special treat. And you know how much your brother loves pizza."

"That's okay," Cameron said quickly. "You don't have to get something special just for me."

The arm around his shoulders loosened, and he could sense her disappointment. "But we want to," she said softly. "Having you here again, where you belong, is worth celebrating."

"Thank you," he said, helplessly.

"And we thought we'd watch that baseball video you liked so much," his father said. "The one about the kid who turned into that terrific pitcher after he broke his arm."

Behind him, Stevie mimed gagging. Out of the corner of his eye, Cameron saw Diana hide a smile. "That's—that's great," he stammered. Had Neil liked baseball? Cameron played in the school yard sometimes. It was okay, but Pop never let him join a Little League team or anything.

Cameron let the woman steer him into the family room. He slipped into a wooden rocking chair, so he wouldn't have to sit too close to anyone. His parents sat in a pair of recliners. The video was okay, but the kids in it seemed so young—as young as Stevie, or younger. Diana and Stevie were clearly bored. Diana sat reading a book, glancing up at the screen only occasionally. Stevie sprawled on the carpet, playing with a collection of plastic action figures. Still, it felt strangely comforting to be part of a family. He could see Neil's parents holding hands between their recliners.

They stopped the video when the pizza came. His mother announced, "We ordered your favorite—sausage and pepperoni, with extra cheese."

Cameron stared at the gooey mess of pizza. Pop never ordered pizza. He didn't want anyone coming to the house if he could help it, even a delivery man. Sometimes Cameron got to eat a slice of frozen pizza, if Pop was feeling generous.

"I hate sausage," Stevie complained.

"Tonight we're having sausage and pepperoni for your brother," his mother said brightly.

"Just pick off the sausage," Diana advised. "It'll taste okay."

Stevie sighed loudly and carried his plate to the kitchen table.

"I thought we'd eat in the family room," his mother said, "so we could finish the video."

Diana and Stevie both stared at her. "You never let us eat there," Stevie said finally.

"Well, it's a special night," his mother said.

"I know," Diana said, her voice flat. "Neil's home."

Cameron watched her carry her pizza to the family room. He tried to take only one small slice, but his mother piled two large ones on his plate.

"I've got the drinks for everybody," his father said. "We got root beer for you, Neil."

He could tell from the expression in the man's voice that root beer must have been Neil's favorite. "Thanks," he said.

Stevie poked him. "Hey—what's a tree's favorite drink?"

Cameron stared at the boy. What was it with the kid? Had Neil collected riddles or something? How could he figure out all of them?

His father smiled. "Neil probably doesn't even remember all those old riddles, Stevie."

"Why not?" Stevie asked.

Cameron looked at the glass the man had handed him, and thought about the riddle again. He groaned inwardly at the pun. "I remember," he said, and raised the glass, pretending to toast the boy. "Trees drink root beer."

Stevie nodded, and Cameron followed the boy into the family room, relieved that he'd guessed right. But what would happen when Stevie came up with a riddle he couldn't guess?

He tried to choke down the pizza, but the sausage

was too spicy, and the cheese was so thick and rubbery he could barely chew it or swallow it. He tried to wash it down with root beer, but the drink was cloying. He was used to water, and a Coke sometimes, as a treat when Pop was in a good mood or as a reward for good behavior. But he was afraid to stop, afraid they'd be angry with him after they'd gone to so much trouble, afraid they'd be suspicious. He kept doggedly chewing, and smiling at his parents, who were watching him more than the video.

Finally he gave up. Neil probably never went to bed early, but Cameron couldn't keep acting any longer, and he thought if he ate another bite he would throw up. "I'm sorry," he said. "I'm just so tired. Would it be okay if I went to bed?"

Diana's eyes widened. Stevie said, "I don't have to go to bed, do I? It's not even my bedtime yet!"

His father said, "No, you can stay up like normal, Stevie. But Neil's had a hard day."

Cameron breathed a faint sigh of relief. "Thank you," he said softly. He carefully carried his plate and the glass still half full of root beer to the kitchen. Behind him he heard someone stop the video and switch channels. He heard explosions on the television, and thought he heard Stevie laugh. He didn't care what they wanted to watch. He just had to be alone and get some sleep.

But the new pajamas on his bed felt stiff, and Cameron lay in the darkness, unable to fall asleep. He felt drained, but he also felt twisted taut inside. Could he pull it off? How many mistakes had he made that day alone? Those stupid riddles...And he should have eaten more of the pizza. He should have watched the movie through to the end. Were they talking about him in the other room, analyzing his mistakes? He had to do better tomorrow—he wanted to stay here, more than he'd wanted anything in his life. He thought he'd just wanted to survive, but he remembered the sight of Neil's parents holding hands. What would it be like to really belong to a family where people held hands and looked at each other with affection instead of—

Cameron opened his eyes quickly to shut out the memory of Pop's smile, and saw a movement in the doorway. He shut his eyes immediately, then opened them just enough to look through his lashes. He could make out a figure standing there—Neil's mother, her arms folded across her chest. He breathed slowly, hoping she'd think he was already asleep and leave him alone. Then he heard footsteps in the hallway.

"Is he asleep?" his father asked in a low voice. Apparently Stevie and Diana had been abandoned.

"Shhh," his mother whispered. She leaned against the man, and he put his arms around her.

"It's going to be all right, Annie," he said softly. "He's home now."

"Do you think he liked the pizza?" she asked. "And the video? He didn't eat very much, and he didn't watch the end."

They did notice, he thought, with a sickening jolt.

But the man only said, "He was worn out. It's going to take him time to adjust. We have to give him that time."

"And what about the riddles?" She sounded worried. "He was always crazy about those silly riddles—" Her voice caught.

The man sighed. "Riddles are fine for Stevie now, and for Neil then. But he's a lot older. I'm sure they're not important to him anymore."

"I know, I know." But she didn't sound as if she believed it. "It just seems as if he'd remember them, at least. When Stevie asked him, he acted like he'd never heard the riddles before."

"Annie," the man said slowly, "you've got to accept there are going to be things he doesn't remember. They may come back to him later on, but there may be some things he'll never remember. Riddles aren't the most important memories we want him to recover."

"Of course not—it just seemed strange. That's all." Her tone was sad.

The man didn't answer, and the two of them stood silently, holding each other, just watching him. Cameron was afraid to move, for fear they'd realize he'd been awake all along.

At last his mother said, "It's past Stevie's bedtime. I'll get him." But she stood there a moment longer before turning and walking back down the hall, leaving the man alone.

"I'm not tired," Stevie mumbled a moment later.

"Shhh. Here, honey, get into your pajamas," his mother urged him softly.

"You've had a long day, too," his father said, helping the boy change.

"But I'm not tired," Stevie whined.

"I know," his father said. He helped the boy into bed and pulled the covers over him. "Good night, Stevie."

The boy yawned. "Good night, Daddy."

Cameron watched his father bend down, and stopped breathing. The man kissed the boy briefly, then stood, and his mother stooped over him. In a moment, the boy's breathing turned steady.

Then she came to his bed. Cameron let his eyelashes fall. He heard Pop's warning and felt his body stiffen. *Don't struggle. Be good, and everything will be all right.* He made himself lie there motionless as she bent over him and kissed his cheek.

"Good night, Neil," she said gently, as if the words were a prayer.

Then he felt the man bending over him. *Don't struggle. Don't make a sound.* His lips brushed Cameron's forehead.

Finally the footsteps left the room, and Cameron let himself slide into exhausted sleep.

Heart pounding, he was suddenly, fully awake. Motionless, eyes closed, he listened for the sound that had awakened him. Stevie's breathing continued light and even—that wasn't it. Then he heard the floor by his bed creak, followed by a sigh. He forced himself not to move, and waited to feel the weight on the bed.

It didn't come.

Carefully Cameron eased his eyelids open just enough to peer through his lashes. Moonlight fell on the man's figure standing at the foot of the bed. Head bent to one side, he stood slumped, his hands in the pockets of his robe. Cameron waited, torn between fear and hope that the man would take Pop's place.

Finally the figure straightened, and Cameron held his breath.

"Sleep well, son. You're safe now." The voice was barely a whisper. Then the man turned and left.

Cameron opened his eyes and stared at the shadows dancing on the far wall. Was he truly safe? Without Pop, would he ever be safe again?

7

Sibling Rivalry

"So why did you do it?" Diana asked.

His fingers froze on the straps of the life jacket. His whole body went absolutely still, the way it had when Pop came upon him unexpectedly. *She knows*, Cameron thought. *She knows who I am, and she's asking why I said I was Neil. What do I do now?*

The lake shimmered in front of him, blinding in the sunlight. Both small boats were assembled and rigged now, and he needn't have worried about remembering how to sail. His father's refresher course had explained everything.

"I don't care if you think you remember," the man had said, his voice patient but firm. "I'm not letting you go out on the lake until we've gone over every piece of the sailboat together, and assembled it, and taken it apart, and put it back together again."

His mother had sat at the redwood picnic table, never taking her eyes off him, and that made him clumsy at first. But after a while he'd managed to concentrate on the boat, and lost himself in the pleasure of handling the pieces of the Sunfish. He liked the smooth aluminum and fiberglass under his hands, and he liked the neat way the pieces slid together and locked into place. He liked the flapping sound of the sail as it hung loose, luffing in the breeze after he'd rigged it but not tightened it before launching the boat.

Diana sat at the picnic table, too, at the end farthest from her mother. She glanced up at Cameron now and then, but mostly read her book. Stevie seemed to have disappeared after complaining that he didn't like waffles with strawberry jam and wanted plain syrup instead. Cameron had been about to agree with him when his mother had said, "I'm sorry, Stevie. Strawberry jam is Neil's favorite. But I'll get the syrup for you."

What if he'd asked for the syrup first? They would have all stared at him. But *strawberry jam is Neil's favorite—and you can't remember the riddles— You can't be Neil!* Would they have called Detective Simmons? Cameron knew the detective would have been only too happy to rush over and arrest him. He was probably just waiting for the chance. If Stevie hadn't said something, Cameron would have slipped up before the day had barely begun. Cameron had lost his appetite at that point, along with Stevie. But the younger boy just left the table. Cameron had to stay and eat the waffles, thick with strawberry jam, even though they tasted like slimy

Styrofoam, and smile because the others were watching him. It had been a relief to get outside, where his father didn't expect him to remember anything, and a relief to listen to the list of rules the man had laid out for him.

"I don't want you to go out sailing unless Diana goes in her boat, also," he'd said. "And you can't go out unless you wear your life jacket. No discussion about these rules, all right?"

Cameron agreed at once. His father couldn't know that having to wear the life jacket was an added relief. It hid the fact that he was wearing a shirt instead of just his swimming trunks. Cameron didn't care how much Dr. Oshida had told them, he didn't want anyone to see his back. Anyway, he didn't mind rules. They told him what to do to prevent punishment, to prove that he was good at last, even if he could never be good enough. Each one of Neil's father's rules helped diminish Cameron's fear of being found out through something like the syrup or the jokes, and laid another brick in the wall of safety he could feel going up around himself.

The wall Diana seemed to be trying to knock down.

Cameron released the clasp on the life jacket and turned to face her. "What?" he asked, keeping his voice even, the way he did whenever a teacher asked him something in school.

"Why did you go off in the mall that day?" she asked roughly, and he realized she wasn't challenging his claim to be Neil after all.

The articles had said that Neil had gotten impatient while his mother was shopping in a big department store in the mall. She told him to wait, but Neil sneaked away and went off by himself. They knew he'd gone into the record store, because the clerk there recognized his picture; she said he'd started hanging around the videotape section, so she'd told him to go find his mom. The teenager giving prizes in the video game arcade recognized his picture, too, and said that the boy had left with his father. He said that before he realized that the man hadn't been the boy's father, but he couldn't say what the man looked like. He was paid to keep an eye on the kids, he said, not the grown-ups.

"Why did you go off with that man?" Diana demanded, and Cameron could hear the anger clearly in her voice this time. "Why did you ruin everything?"

"I didn't mean—" he began, staring at her helplessly. *Why had Neil done it, any of it?* It was a stupid thing to do, going off with a stranger. Yet all the boys had done it, one way or another. Why would a kid go off alone in a mall in the first place, anyway? Then he thought of what it must have been like with toddler Stevie demanding attention, and six-year-old Diana tagging along.

"I just wanted to be alone for a while," he said, imagining what Neil must have felt. "I thought I was old enough to go by myself."

"Well, you weren't," Diana snapped.

He shook his head.

"You should have waited," she told him. "Mom said she'd take all of us to the arcade—"

"I didn't want everybody," he said suddenly, betting that was what Neil had felt.

Her lips twisted in a sneer. "You never did," she said. "It must really bum you that you have to room with Stevie again, and you can't even go sailing without me. You never wanted to waste time with us. Stevie practically worshiped you, but you never had any time for him— you ordered him around, or you told him to get lost."

"I—"

"So you got your own way, like always," she went on, ignoring him. "You went off by yourself, and you got your wish—you sure got away from us for a long time. But why did you have to spoil everything for the rest of us?"

Cameron stared at her blankly. Surely Neil had spoiled everything for himself, not her. She was still alive, she lived in this great house, she had parents, friends, a sailboat, an allowance. She didn't know what Hank Miller was like.

"What are you talking about?" he said, suddenly angry himself. "You're safe! You don't have any idea what I—"

"You!" she shouted, and they both suddenly glanced toward the house to make sure no one was watching their fight. But apparently their parents had left them alone, as they'd promised. "Some time to get to know each other again," Neil's father had said. Cameron supposed that was what they were doing, all right.

Diana went on in a quieter voice. All the anger and pain were still there, but they didn't carry any further than Cameron's ears. "That's what it's always come down to—*you*! You never cared about anybody but yourself. If Mom and Dad weren't paying attention to you, you were furious. Well, you ought to be delighted. You're all anybody's been thinking about for the past six years!"

"I've been gone," he told her. "You've been here!"

"So what?" she said, her eyes blinking dangerously. "Stevie and I were here, so they didn't have to worry about us. It was all Neil—'Where's Neil?' Put the posters up, ask everybody at the mall, drive up and down the streets, look for you—look everywhere for *you*. Talk to the police, call the task force, talk to a psychic, give another interview, in case somebody has seen you and might remember something if they see your picture—you, you, YOU!"

"But—" he tried to say, but he couldn't stop her.

"I had the lead in our fourth-grade play," she went on, and he could see now that she was crying. "They promised to come, they said it was great, they were so proud of me. Then that special investigator assigned to your case called because he'd had another report of a missing boy from the same mall, and this time they had some information about a car or something."

Her voice was choked now. "They never came to my play. You were all they cared about. They went to work, they talked to the police, and they didn't have any time left over for Stevie and me."

She stared hard at him, the tears still running down her face. "And they're still doing it. Dad tells you all about sailing, Mom makes sure you get your favorite food. They tell Stevie not to wake you up this morning—and it's his room, too. They tell us to be careful

with you because you've been through such an ordeal—well, what about us? What about *our* ordeal?"

"I'm sorry!" he cried, finally succeeding in breaking
into her outpouring. "I'm sorry—I don't care if you believe me or not—that's not what I wanted to happen!"

As Cameron said it, he wondered whether, just
maybe, that had been what Neil had wanted, if he really
was the selfish little jerk Diana had described. But no
kid would be willing to suffer the way Neil had suf-
fered, just to be so important to his family. He probably
hadn't realized what he was doing when he tried to get
his parents' attention, or when he went to the arcade
alone that afternoon. He was too little, or too dumb, to
understand consequences. Well, Pop had taught Cameron all about consequences. The ache inside filled him
again, and he wished he were back with Pop, back where
the rules were clearer, where he understood the penal-
ties better, and where he could at least dream of learning to be good enough someday to make the beatings
stop. He didn't think Neil could ever be good enough
to win Diana's approval.

"I don't want anybody's attention," Cameron told her,
fighting to control his inner shaking. "I just want to be
left alone."

"Fine with me," Diana said, turning away and scrub-
bing the tears from her face with the back of her hand.
"But I've got to act like I'm glad you're home, or Dad
will be disappointed in me. I've got to hang around here
with you. I'm missing tryouts for the summer musi-
cal—they're doing *The Sound of Music,* and I know I'd

get a good part. I want to be an actress, but Dad doesn't care about me. All he's ever cared about is you."

Cameron felt bludgeoned, the way he'd felt when Pop had told him how bad he was. Diana might not know he wasn't Neil, but she already knew he was a disappointment.

"Just remember—once school starts you're on your own," she went on. Then she turned back suddenly, her eyes narrowed. "What grade are you going into, anyway?"

Cameron looked out at the sparkling water, trying to blank out her dislike. "Eighth," he said. "I got held back."

"No!" Her voice was outraged. "That's too much!"

"What?"

"I'm going into eighth grade, too!" Diana cried. "But I won't be stuck with you all the time! It's bad enough everybody's going to be all amazed at your coming back—I refuse to have you in my class!"

"Don't worry," he said stiffly. "The last place I want to be is in your class."

She dragged the straps of her life jacket angrily through the clasps and started for the dock. Then she stopped and turned back to him. "If you went to school and everything," she demanded, "why didn't you tell anybody who you were? A teacher, or the police? Why did you go along with him?"

Cameron stared at her for a minute, then looked back down at the straps dangling limply from his own life jacket. Carefully he threaded one through the clasp.

Why did everybody think he could have said some-thing? Why weren't they angry at the adults who were free, who weren't being beaten and punished, who must have seen but who hadn't done anything all the times he'd been bruised and dizzy and swallowing aspirin every hour? Sure, he'd tried to hide it, but grown-ups were supposed to be smarter than kids—why hadn't they seen through him and helped him? Why was he to blame for everything? He wanted to shout at her, to shake her, but he couldn't let himself be like Pop.

His arms felt heavy as he smoothed out the second strap. "He told me not to," he said quietly. "He told me he'd kill me if I didn't do what he said."

"But if you'd told somebody, they'd have arrested him and he couldn't have done anything to you."

Cameron fastened the last clasp and raised his eyes to meet her angry glare. "I had to do what he said. He killed all the other boys who didn't do what he told them to."

Then he walked past her unsteadily and climbed into the bobbing Sunfish. After a minute she stepped into her own boat and cast off.

8

Shadow of the Past

No, Cameron tried to say. *Don't go with him!* But the boy went, slipping his hand into the man's. He skipped alongside the man, looking up eagerly as he talked.

Then they were in the house, and Cameron said, "Be good, keep quiet. If you just do what he says, you'll make it, like me."

But the boy wouldn't listen. He tossed his jacket on the floor, he climbed on the furniture. He talked and he laughed, and when the man yelled at him, he began to cry.

"Stop it!" Cameron told him, shaking the boy. "Don't cry! He doesn't like it when you cry!"

But it was too late. The man opened the cellar door and gave Cameron a shove, and as he tumbled down the stairs he could hear the man unbuckling his belt and cursing.

With a strangled sob Cameron sat upright and found himself not on the hardpacked earth floor of the cellar, but in a twin bed in a sunfilled room. The sheets were damp and twisted around him, and Stevie was staring at him curiously, his dark hair still sleep-tousled.

"What were you dreaming about?" he asked. "You sounded like you were trying to say something, but nothing came out."

Cameron wasn't surprised. Pop had taught him how to keep silent early on. He jerked at the sheets and freed himself, then shivered slightly in the air-conditioning. "I was dreaming about the man who took me," he said shortly. Then he looked at the smaller boy, who frowned back at him under his thick tangle of dark hair: Neil's brother.

"Listen," he said. "Don't ever go anywhere with a stranger, Stevie. Run away from him."

Stevie scrunched up his face. "I know that. You think I don't know that? Mom and Dad have told me about a million times."

Cameron sighed. "Well, don't forget it, okay? It's really important."

Stevie shrugged. He climbed out of bed and dragged off his pajamas, then pulled on shorts and picked up a faded surfing T-shirt. "Hey—why didn't the ocean say hello?"

Cameron closed his eyes. He didn't know how long he could keep trying to think up riddle answers. Why was the boy asking about the ocean, anyway? Cameron thought of the surfing T-shirt, and grinned. He opened his eyes. "Because it waved."

Stevie actually grinned back, just for a moment. Then he said, "Come on. Mom told Mrs. Pierson to make pancakes for you, and it's late."

Mrs. Pierson had been the housekeeper before Neil disappeared; Cameron remembered that from the articles. She came on weekdays, when Mrs. Lacey was at the museum and Mr. Lacey was at his law office. Cameron wondered what she'd expect him to be like.

He sat in his bed and looked around the room, half of it cluttered with Stevie's toys and half of it eerily bare in contrast. He wondered if any of the books or games on Stevie's side of the room had belonged to Neil once. Had the Laceys saved Neil's things, hoping he would come home, then finally realized that even if he did he'd be too old for them? What had they done with the things then? Thrown them away? Saved them for Stevie?

Even if he could have gotten back into his own house, there was nothing Cameron would have taken with him. He'd never had toys, like the other kids in school had. He'd used school bats when he played ball at recess, and the books he'd read had all been from the library or from school. Had Pop ever given him anything except clothes? Cameron didn't think so, but maybe he just didn't remember. No birthday presents—he had a birthday set down on the school records, but Pop never acknowledged it when the day came. No Christmas presents, either. Santa had been a larger-than-life version of Pop, knowing whether he'd been bad or good. Cameron had always been too bad to be given presents. It had been a relief to be sure that Santa was only a made-up story.

He punched the sweat-soaked pillow angrily. He had no memories, no souvenirs of growing up. Between the amnesia and his jail-like existence, Pop had stolen his past. Cameron glared at the room around him. Well, now he was getting even by stealing Neil's future.

He slid out of bed and walked unsteadily into the bathroom. He stripped off his sweaty pajamas and stepped into the shower, wishing he could wash away the dream and the exhaustion he felt even after sleeping late. He'd lain awake the night before, listening to Stevie's soft, steady breathing, thinking how hard it was to guess the right thing to do or say, like stepping blindly out into space and hoping there was a step there to catch you—like going into dinner in the dining room Tuesday night. It was the first time they'd eaten there, and Cameron had a bad moment when he saw the places set at the table: one chair at either end for the adults, then two chairs on one side and only one on the other. Everyone was waiting for him to sit down, and Cameron's appetite for the roast had died as he realized they expected him to sit in Neil's regular place. But which one was it?

His mind raced—would the two boys sit on one side, and Diana on the other? Or would the two older kids sit together, so Stevie could sit all alone where he could make a mess? Cameron felt his feet move him closer to the table, and he suddenly walked steadily to the solitary chair, gambling that Diana had been right about Neil. The kid she described would have wanted to sit by himself. And that chair faced the window, looking out at the lake. As Cameron pulled the chair out and slipped into it, he made himself look up to read the judgment in the Laceys' faces. From his mother's smile, he could tell he'd chosen right.

For every right choice, though, how many wrong ones had he made, or almost made? He'd been there only a day and a half. How many days could he do this? How could he work so hard every day of the next three and a half years, until he was eighteen and could look after himself? It *was* hard work, trying to live someone else's life, harder than digging in the cellar. Was he strong enough to do it day after day?

Breakfast wasn't only pancakes with Mrs. Pierson. His parents were there, too, waiting for him so they could eat. Cameron made himself smile at them and let Mrs. Pierson hug him, then slipped into the only empty chair at the round table, relieved not to have to choose which one should be Neil's. His wary glance at the table saw only syrup, so he figured that was what Neil liked on his pancakes. Maybe today would be easier. He sat down quickly, apologizing for being late, and took a bite so the others would start on their own meal. When he told the housekeeper how good the pancakes were, she looked pleased.

He glanced cautiously at his parents. His father was wearing a suit, but his mother wore slacks and a loose top, and her golden hair was tied back. Surely she didn't dress like that at the museum?

She smiled at him, and he realized his uncertainty must have shown on his face. "I thought I'd stay home with you again today, Neil. We need to take you shopping for some new clothes—you can't live in that shirt and jeans!"

He remembered how Pop had complained about the cost of clothes, and wondered how he'd be expected to pay for the clothes here. "I'm sorry," he said.

"Nothing to be sorry about," his father said, dragging a forkful of pancakes through the syrup puddled on his plate. "Your mother still loves to go shopping as much as ever."

"And it's been so long since I've been able to buy you anything," she said, her voice catching.

Cameron looked down at his plate, the pancakes settling heavily in his stomach.

"Diana, Stevie," his father said, "are you two going along to help your mother and brother buy out the mall?"

Diana shook her head. "No, thanks. I don't have any allowance left."

"Me, neither," said Stevie.

So the kids must pay for their own things, Cameron realized. He wondered how they earned their allowances—how he would be expected to earn his.

"You've both been big spenders, eh?" His father chuckled. "Well, it's a special occasion—we can spring for some extra summer stuff for you, too."

His mother looked a little disappointed. Cameron realized she must have wanted to spend the time alone with him. He wasn't sure whether he wanted the others to come along to distract her, or whether it would be easier if it were just the two of them. It turned out not to matter what he wanted, though. Diana saw her mother's expression and said, "That's okay. I don't need anything. I'll just stay here and read."

Stevie said, "I want to play on the computer."

"It sounds like it's just the two of us," his mother said quickly.

So Cameron let her take him to a crowded mall, where at least no one paid any attention to him except her. Terrified of making a mistake, he watched her closely and followed her lead in everything from the car radio (she told him he could pick the station, and he saw a smile cross her face when the dial paused on a station with loud music. "You still like that horrible stuff, don't you?") to what color T-shirts to buy ("Let's see, is red still your favorite color? How about this one with the clipper ship on it—you still love those tall ships, don't you?") to what to choose for lunch at the mall food court ("You can still eat plate after plate of those nachos smothered in fake cheese, I'll bet.").

The worst moment came when they looked at a rack of windbreakers and she said, "Here—you pick what you want, Neil. I've been choosing everything for you!" He reached instinctively for a clear blue jacket the color of the lake on a sunny day, and she said, "I was so sure you'd choose the black one. You always thought a black jacket was so cool."

Cameron froze. Now the accusation would come. *You can't be Neil—who are you?* But he couldn't make himself pick up the black one. Pop had a black jacket. He didn't think he could wear a jacket like Pop's. "This one looks like the lake," he said finally. "Would it be okay if I got it, instead?"

He held his breath, but she only said, "Of course! I want you to have whatever you want, honey. It's okay if you want to choose something different." She paused a moment, then added, "You're not eight anymore." But she sounded reluctant to admit it.

Finally she was spent, and he was relieved. He'd passed embarrassment at how much she'd bought him at least an hour earlier, and now felt actively guilty at taking so much from the Laceys. They walked by a video arcade on the way back to the car, and he couldn't help wondering if this was the same mall where Neil had been abducted. She didn't say anything, though, and so he kept his eyes straight ahead and followed her to the parking lot, lugging the overstuffed department store bags.

By the time they got home, he was exhausted from the effort of picking up on her hints and fearing that he'd do something so un-Neil-like that she'd realize the truth. How was he going to act the way the Laceys expected Neil to behave day after day? He could only hope that they'd ultimately decide their son had grown up and accept Cameron as they'd have accepted the fourteen-year-old Neil, but he didn't know if that would ever happen.

Diana came to watch them carry in the bags of clothes, her book under one arm. "I'd have come with you if I knew you were going to buy out the mall for real," she said. "I thought it was just an expression."

"I wish you had come," her mother said. "Have some dessert with us. I had Mrs. Pierson make chocolate cake."

Cameron didn't have to ask if that was Neil's favorite.

"I know," Diana said. "She wouldn't let Stevie or me eat any of it until you got home."

"Well, you can have some now," her mother said. She served Cameron a huge piece, and then gave Diana a smaller one. "You two enjoy—I'm going to call the office and make sure they're managing without me."

Cameron waited until she was gone. "Here," he said. "You can have the big piece. It's too much for me."

"No way," Diana said. "She'd notice, and blame me for bullying you."

"You didn't," he said.

"I know. But it wouldn't make any difference."

Cameron was too tired to argue. Once Diana licked the last of the frosting off her fork and left the table, he chewed mechanically for a while, in case his mother came back in. Then he scraped the rest of the cake down the garbage disposal, rinsed off his plate, and escaped to the dock, where he was too tired to track down Diana so he could go sailing. It was enough to look at the boat bobbing in the water, and to know he could escape into it if he wanted to.

He made it through the evening, finding it easier now that he knew where to sit and could guess Stevie's riddles. But the next morning when he awoke to find the twisted blanket squeezing him, not Pop, Cameron had to remind himself all over again that he was Neil now, and he was safe—as long as the Laceys believed him, anyway.

Mrs. Pierson was making bacon and eggs. She put a plate of sunny-side-up eggs in front of him as Cameron slid into his chair. "Just the way you like them," she said, beaming.

Cameron looked at the bright yellow runny yolks and felt his stomach clench. "Thanks," he managed. "They look great."

His father set aside the paper and smiled at him. "So—what do you have planned for today?"

Cameron saw Diana eyeing the paper curiously. "Sailing," he said. "If it's okay with Diana, I mean."

His father chuckled, and Diana sighed. "I'm not going to live on the lake all summer, you know." Then her father caught her eye, and she shrugged. "But sure—we can go sailing today, if you like."

"Good," her mother said. "Then I'm going to pick up some donations for the museum."

Stevie grinned. "Then the computer's all mine," he crowed.

His father groaned. "We've got to wean you from that machine before you start sprouting computer cables instead of hair."

"Cyberkid," teased Diana, and they all laughed. Cameron felt a bright flash of pleasure at the way his laughter blended with theirs.

"Okay, okay," Stevie said. "I'll play outside in the morning, and then get on the computer this afternoon, okay?"

"It's a start," his father said.

Cameron wondered why Stevie didn't ever sail with them.

Then his mother hugged him tightly and went to get ready to leave. His father picked up the newspaper and left the table, telling them to have a nice sail. And Stevie crammed a whole piece of bacon into his mouth and slid off his chair.

Diana looked around to make sure they had the kitchen to themselves, then leaned closer to him. "You made the front page of the local paper. Dad took it with him, but I saw it first. There's the picture of you when you were eight, and an article all about your turning up at the police station and everything."

"So?" he asked, cringing inside and wondering why she'd brought it up.

"So you're pretty definitely alive," Diana said around a mouthful of bacon. "What about the guy they arrested two years ago for killing you?" she demanded triumphantly.

Cameron set his fork down in the runny egg yolk and stared at her. "What guy?" he whispered.

Diana groaned. "Oh, come off it. I don't buy this amnesia stuff the doctor was talking about. And even if you can't remember everything you've got to remember this. The cops came and talked to you about it while you were still with that man Miller. I don't know why you didn't tell them who you were—he couldn't have killed you if the cops were protecting you."

"I remember," Cameron said dully, staring at the egg-smeared plate and feeling sick.

Mrs. Pierson suddenly appeared with fresh bacon, and Diana changed the subject, talking about sailing. When her mother came in to say good-bye again, Diana told her, "You go to work every day, Mom—it's not such a big deal."

The housekeeper shushed Diana as her mother hugged Cameron again, then went around the table to give Diana a perfunctory hug as well.

"Bye," Diana said impatiently. As soon as the car pulled out of the garage, she jumped up from the table, grabbed her dishes, and carried them into the kitchen, then went outside.

Cameron heard the side door slam as he managed to choke down the last of his eggs and some more bacon. Then Mrs. Pierson sat down beside him with a cup of coffee and a hungry expression on her face. Cameron thanked her for the breakfast, then got up from the table with his own dishes, leaving her the last of the bacon even though he didn't think that was what she was hungry for.

He found Diana sitting at the redwood picnic table outside. "So what did the paper say about that guy?" he asked without preamble.

She shrugged.

"Come on," he said. "What happened to him?"

She looked up at him. "Why do you care?"

Cameron watched the lake, glass-smooth in the calm morning. The sailboats rested quietly beside the dock. He could see Stevie sitting in the larger family boat, a life jacket on over his T-shirt, gazing out across the water. Cameron tried to make his mind blank and peaceful. But he had to ask, "Did he go to jail?"

"Of course."

"But not for killing me," he said quickly.

She chuckled unkindly. "So it seems now."

He shrugged. "Okay, have it your way. I'll ask Mom and Dad when they get home." Calling them that still felt strange in his mouth.

Diana drummed her fingers on the table. "They thought he'd killed you, and a lot of the other boys, but I don't think they could prove it."

"So what did he go to jail for?"

"For something else, another boy." She sighed. "I'm not sure, I only know that he was involved with Hank Miller."

He sure was, Cameron thought, remembering the man Pop had called Cougar. He was hardly a man, really. He wasn't much more than a boy himself.

"You want to find out more?" she asked abruptly.

He looked at her. "How?"

A slow smile crossed her face. "Dad took the paper before I could finish the article, but I know where we can find out about him."

"Where?" He needed to know, he realized suddenly. Pop was gone, but Cougar was apparently still alive. Deep inside, Cameron couldn't help wishing it were the other way around.

She stood up. "The library. They won't have just today's paper, they'll have the papers from when the guy was arrested, too."

"Would Mom take us?" he asked.

Diana laughed. "You don't think I wait to go to the library until Mom's around, do you? She sure doesn't stay home on weekdays for Stevie and me! I just bike over whenever I want a new book." She measured him with her eyes. "You're small enough to use Stevie's new bike. Don't worry—it'll just be for today. I'm sure Mom and Dad will get you a new one. I can't imagine why Mom didn't buy you one when you went shopping."

Cameron ignored the edge in her voice and followed her to the garage, more worried about how he was going to explain his inability to ride a bike. All kids knew how to ride bikes. Could he get away with blaming this on the amnesia?

9

Cougar

Cameron stared dubiously at the green-and-black bike Diana had wheeled up to him.

She returned with a turquoise racing bike and laughed at him. "Come on, surely you haven't forgotten how to ride a bike?"

"I haven't ridden one for a long time," he said. He took a deep breath, threw one leg over the seat, and rested his right foot on the pedal.

"Okay?" she asked.

"Okay," he said, wondering how much it would hurt to fall off the bike. Less than Pop's hands and belt, anyway. The wheels wobbled frantically, but to his surprise, he juggled his weight from side to side, compensating, and pedaled jerkily.

"Like they say," Diana said, surprising him so much he almost lost his balance all over again, "you never forget how to ride a bike."

Or some people are just fast learners, Cameron thought thankfully as he followed her. He wondered if he had ridden a bike sometime in the past. Maybe he had, and Pop had forbidden it. If Pop had beaten him for it, he might have blanked out learning how. There were so many things he knew he should remember, but couldn't.

Luckily the Freeport library wasn't too far away. By the time Cameron coasted up to the bike rack behind Diana, he was beginning to feel more confident about the machine. But every time he heard a car pass by he jumped, jerking the handlebars and nearly losing control. He couldn't get the idea out of his head that being here with the Laceys wasn't for real—the police had just made it up about killing Pop, and any minute he'd feel Pop's fingers digging into his shoulder. Part of him wanted that to be true so he could go back home, but the part of him that wanted to be Neil Lacey knew that if Pop showed up he'd give Cameron the worst punishment of his life for trying to escape. Cameron was only too glad to climb off the bike before he lost control by jumping at shadows and made a real fool out of himself.

Diana threaded her chain through both bikes and the rack, and led the way up the stairs into the library.

He followed her into the cool foyer, forgetting about Cougar for the moment, just glad that they'd come. He'd always loved libraries, even when he'd been a really slow reader. Books were a good way of not thinking about things, almost as good a way of blanking out reality as escaping to the sailboat in his mind. Pop hadn't cared if he read a book, as long as he dropped it when ordered. Reading was quiet, and that's what Pop had liked.

"This is my brother Neil," Diana announced, shattering his thoughts.

Cameron found himself staring at two wide-eyed librarians on the other side of the checkout desk. Up until now he'd been an expert on not being noticed, but apparently Diana had no interest in keeping a low profile. He wished he could dissolve into the shadows.

"He needs a new library card," Diana went on, looking pleased with the stunned silence she had created.

"Hi," he told the two women weakly.

"Come on," Diana said, pulling him away by one sleeve before the librarians could say anything. "We'll pick up your card when we're ready to check out books."

"Why did you do that?" he muttered, jerking his sleeve loose.

"What?" she asked, looking innocent.

"Make a scene like that?"

Diana turned to him. "You used to always run up to the front desk and say hi—you liked that even more than checking out books. You always liked being the center of attention."

Cameron met her stare, not caring what Neil would do. "Not anymore. So quit it." She looked surprised, and he went on, "Where are the old newspapers, anyway?"

She grinned then. "They don't keep old newspapers, dummy. It's all on microfilm."

She led him to a weird machine with a wide screen,

an empty spindle, an empty take-up reel, and a handle for turning them. It sat on a table in the center of the main reading room.

"Wait here, if you don't want a fuss," she told him, and disappeared through a door in the far wall.

Cameron looked around nervously and found a similar machine in a corner. He was waiting there when Diana returned in a few minutes with a stack of small boxes.

"You really can't take the limelight," she said, smiling crookedly.

Cameron shook his head but didn't say anything. He couldn't bring himself to explain that he couldn't stand having his back exposed to half the room like that. He'd be looking over his shoulder every time somebody walked behind him.

"Want to read about yourself?" she asked when he said nothing. Cameron shook his head emphatically. He already knew what those articles would say, and he didn't want to read them on a screen. He also didn't want Diana to read them over his shoulder, and maybe make the connection that he only knew the things about Neil that were in the articles.

"I want to read about the man who went to jail," he told her more firmly than he felt. Cameron studied the pile of boxes dubiously. He'd pictured stacks of yellowing newspapers, or lots of newspaper clippings in file folders, like the ones he'd memorized. He felt unnerved by this strange machine.

"Okay," Diana said. She opened one of the boxes,

deftly slipped the reel onto the empty spindle, and threaded it through the machine and into the take-up reel. Then she switched on the power, and Cameron saw a miniature newspaper spread out on the screen. The print was small, but he could make it out clearly enough.

"The boxes are dated," she told him. "They arrested the man about two years ago, so the articles should start in this box." She showed him how to scroll the newspaper pages through the reader. "I'll take back these earlier films if you're sure you don't want to read about yourself."

"I'm positive," he said, scrolling forward until a grainy photograph of Cougar caught his eye, and he shivered involuntarily. Pop hadn't let Cougar do anything to him, although Cameron knew they'd shared some of the other boys. But his stomach lurched as he remembered the two men drinking and laughing. He'd felt Cougar's fist a few times hard on the side of his head when Pop wasn't looking. He remembered Cougar, all right—he remembered the shifting eyes, part mean and part scared, but mostly mean. The paper said his real name was Bill Scott, and he'd been on and off the un- employment rolls since he'd dropped out of high school. He'd been working as a part-time clerk in a liquor store, but he must have lied about his age—he was only nineteen when he was arrested.

Cameron stared at the caption beneath the photo- graph, so paralyzed by memories that he could barely breathe. Cougar had been arrested because of the boy

Pop had let him take. He remembered that night, hearing the two men quarrel. Cougar had been with Pop when they'd picked up the boy—Alan Wells was his name. Pop had been telling the boy what to do, but Cougar kept trying to take charge. Finally Pop had told him to take the kid and get lost—he never wanted to hear from him again. And Cougar had hauled the boy out to his pickup and roared away, spitting gravel from the drive so hard it hit the living room windows. Pop had been angry that night. Cameron shut his eyes and tried to blank out the memory of how Pop had taken out his fury on him.

Then, a couple of days later, the police had come. Pop had ordered Cameron to be quiet or he'd kill him, and despite what Diana and Detective Simmons thought, Cameron had known the threat was true. He'd sat at the bare wood kitchen table, staring blindly at his world history notes, listening to the rise and fall of voices in the living room until he heard his name.

"Mr. Scott says you have a son, Mr. Miller, name of Cameron. Is he here today, sir?"

He'd felt his stomach tighten into knots and wished he could run down into the cellar and hide in the corner with the file cabinet until the cops left. He remembered all too clearly how Pop had told him the cops would take him away and lock him up because he was so bad. Cameron didn't want them to see him.

"May we speak to him, please, Mr. Miller?"

And Pop had led them into the kitchen, to show them his son doing his homework like a good boy.

The cops had been polite. He'd told them he was Cameron Miller and that he didn't really know the man they were talking about. He'd said that his father called the man Cougar, and that Cougar sometimes came and drank beer with his father, but that Cameron didn't stay up with the men.

The cops had shown him a picture of Alan Wells and asked if he'd ever seen the boy, and Cameron had stared at it, remembering the boy's tears that night and wondering if Cougar had killed him. Neither of the cops had seen past his blank stare and tried to help him. Finally he'd shaken his head and said he didn't think so, and asked softly if it was someone he was supposed to know from school. The cops had gone away a little later, and Pop had slapped him on his sore back and grinned at him, telling him he'd been good for once.

Cameron blinked his eyes, trying to focus on the present instead of the past. Reading the newspaper articles now, he saw that Alan Wells hadn't been killed. He'd gotten away from Bill Scott's house, and run and told the police. *Good for him*, Cameron thought. That was one boy who wasn't in Hank Miller's files.

The articles said that Alan had remembered the license plate of the pickup and described Scott's house. He'd told the police there was another man in an out-of-the-way house, but he hadn't been as clear about that one. They'd arrested Scott, and Alan had identified him. It was Scott who'd told the police about Hank Miller. According to the newspaper, the police had gone to Miller's house but had found no evidence to confirm

Scott's accusations. They'd found a quiet widower with a steady job and a son who went to school regularly and didn't make any trouble. Miller and his son were both open about knowing the man, but they said they knew nothing about Alan Wells, and there was nothing to indicate that they were lying. In a police lineup, Alan Wells had failed to identify Miller. Cameron guessed the boy had been too frightened that night to remember Pop's face clearly.

There had been more than twenty missing boys on the files at that time, and the police had wanted to indict Scott for all of them, despite his insistence that Miller was to blame. His lawyer had said that Scott was a victim, too. He'd been abused by his own father until he left home, and should be in therapy instead of in jail. Cameron shuddered. Cougar, abused? How could you grow up to do something like that to someone else, if it had been done to you?

The headlines in subsequent issues of the newspaper were full of speculation, but in the end Scott had only gone to trial for the abduction of Alan Wells. The prosecution had brought up the other boys in court and the judge had ruled that there was no proof that Cougar had ever had anything to do with nine of them, as he'd been in school in Memphis then, and living at home. But Cougar had no alibi for the other cases, so the jury had heard all about those, including Neil Lacey. They'd sent Bill Scott to jail for what he'd tried to do to the Wells boy, and several jurors said they believed he had killed at least eight of the other boys, including Neil.

Because of that, they'd recommended a much heavier sentence than he'd have gotten for Alan Wells alone.

"Hey, Neil?"

Cameron looked up, startled. It was the first time Diana had actually called him Neil.

She was holding a crisp newspaper, the same issue that their father had taken away from her that morning, he guessed. Her eyes were wide, and she was smiling faintly.

"Bill Scott, you know? Last week, after they killed Hank Miller and started to dig in his cellar..." She looked pale beneath the smile, Cameron realized. Maybe reading about the bodies had jolted her.

"... his lawyer went to court to get him released after they dug up the bodies," she went on. "The lawyer said Scott had said all along it was Hank Miller, that he'd been trying to help that boy get away but the kid panicked and didn't understand what had happened to him. So the lawyer filed an appeal, now that they know Hank Miller's really the one who killed the boys. He asked them to release Scott on bail." Diana looked up from the paper. "I guess he has you to thank."

"For what?" Cameron asked, confused.

"For turning up. He didn't kill you, obviously, and his lawyer said he must have told the truth about not killing the others, because the police found all those bodies at Miller's, where he said they'd be. So the court granted his immediate release, pending that appeal."

She handed the newspaper to him. "You're both free now."

10

The Broken Rule

"Not another word out of you, young lady!" Neil's mother shouted. She glared at Diana. "How many times have I told you never to go off alone without telling anybody where you were? How many?"

"I wasn't alone!" Diana screamed. With her fists on her hips and her deep brown eyes wide and furious, Cameron thought she looked exactly like her mother. "I was with Neil! You never yell if I go somewhere with Stevie, as long as we stay together. I just took Neil to the library, so what's the big deal?"

"Shut up," Cameron muttered to her. He might be shaky on a bicycle or a microfilm machine, but apologizing for breaking a rule he didn't even know existed was something he'd had a lot of experience with. "I'm sorry," he said aloud. "I didn't think. It was my fault, but I'm really sorry."

"How could you?" Neil's mother cried. She gripped his shoulders and shook him. "How could you?"

"It was my idea," Diana shouted. "How was I supposed to know you'd want to come home and have lunch with him? You took him shopping all day yesterday! That's more than you ever did for one of us on a workday!"

"Please," he whispered, not resisting the hands on his shoulders. What in the world was Diana doing? It was crazy to argue back—it just made the punishment worse.

His mother suddenly let go of Cameron and turned to face her daughter. "Don't you talk back to me, Diana," she said, her voice icy. "I want you to go to your room and stay there. We'll talk about this when your father comes home tonight."

"That's not fair!" Diana cried. "What about Neil? I suppose you're going to have lunch with him and fuss over him and forgive him everything and take him out and buy him something else just because he's come back!"

She whirled away, and as her glare passed over him, Cameron saw the sheen of tears in her eyes. Her footsteps thudded down the hall, then her bedroom door slammed.

He felt himself trembling and tried to steady his voice. "Please—it was my fault. I didn't think. I'll never go off again like that—"

"Oh, Neil—" His mother was crying now, the tears running down her cheeks. "I thought my taking time off from work this week would be such a nice treat for us both—and then I get here and you've disappeared again." Her breath was coming in jerks. "It was just like before, and I couldn't stand it."

He swallowed. "I'm sorry," he repeated helplessly.

She threw her arms around him suddenly, and he flinched in surprise. He'd been expecting blows, not this rib-crushing hug. "I couldn't bear to lose you again," she whispered into his hair. "Don't ever go off without telling me or your father or Mrs. Pierson where you're going. Promise me, Neil—promise me!"

"I promise," he said quickly.

He made himself stand passively in her embrace, wishing she'd get on with the beating. Then he realized it would be Neil's father who'd administer the punishment, not her. It was like times when Pop had been angry with him but had not been able to punish him right then. He would tie him up and go to work (he never missed a day of work, just the way he'd never let Cameron miss any school—"Nothing irregular about us," Pop would say, chuckling. "Nothing to draw attention"), and Cameron would have to endure the hours until Pop returned and had the uninterrupted time to teach him his lesson.

"I'll wait in my room," he said softly, as she released him. Then he remembered the tears in Diana's eyes, and her saying that he was always the center of attention. Cameron felt strangely sorry for her and looked up at the woman—at his mother. "It really was my fault," he told her. "Please don't punish Diana. I should take her punishment."

She looked surprised, her eyes still damp and her golden hair disheveled. "Neil—" she began.

"I mean it," he said, and swallowed. "Blame me. She only took me because I asked."

Then he turned and hurried to his room.

He shut the door quietly, unlike Diana, and looked around for Stevie. The room was empty except for the bags of new clothes piled on his desk, and Cameron felt relief wash over him. He methodically unpacked the remaining bags and put the clothes away. Then he walked unsteadily to the far side of the room, to the little hollow between his bed and the wall, and sat with his back against the wall.

He pulled his knees up to his chest and wrapped his arms around them, the way he used to do in the cellar. He laid his head down on his folded arms and closed his eyes. The punishment would come soon enough, he told himself, and felt an odd mixture of relief and fear. Pop had always said he was only punishing him because Cameron was so bad. Pop only did it because he loved him. Cameron knew he deserved the beatings, and part of him had wondered if this family would ever love him enough to punish him. But part of him was afraid of that love, too.

He remembered thinking in the hospital that Mr. Lacey looked like a fair man, and he wondered what a fair punishment would be for breaking a rule like not going off alone. Five strokes with a belt? Ten? It might be worse than a belt, but Cameron didn't think so. But he'd asked for Diana's punishment, too. Twenty strokes with a belt could be hard to stand, especially if the man used the buckle. He wondered why he'd spoken up. It was her own fault, for shouting back. She should have kept quiet and apologized. And she hadn't listened to him when he'd tried to tell her. Just like the boys....

He jumped slightly at a loud knock, then the door burst open.

"Neil?"

He squeezed his knees more tightly and wished she'd go away. Hadn't she heard the order to stay in her room until her father decided on the punishment? No wonder Pop had killed Neil, he thought bitterly. If the boy was anything like his sister, he hadn't had the sense to obey.

"What are you doing hiding down there?"

Her voice sounded funny—confused and apologetic. Cameron raised his head and looked up at her.

Diana stood over him, frowning and chewing her lower lip. "Mom said I didn't have to stay in my room. She's gone in to the museum to sort the new donations after all." She paused. "I figured if I didn't have to stay, you sure didn't."

He shrugged, not bothering to explain that she didn't have to stay because he'd taken on her punishment.

"Why'd you do that?" she asked suddenly.

"What?"

"Tell Mom it was all your fault."

He shrugged again. "Why didn't you shut up, or just say you were sorry?" he asked her.

"But it wasn't fair!" she cried, outraged.

"So?"

She frowned at him. "What do you mean?"

"What does fair have to do with anything?" Cameron tried to explain. "Grown-ups—they do what they want. They make the rules and they set the punishments, and it's stupid to argue." He shuddered, thinking of what Pop would have done with her—not that Pop cared much about girls, but still. "You follow the rules, and if you break them you apologize and know you'll get punished, and you take the punishment and keep quiet and don't cry."

She didn't say anything for a while, then sat down cross-legged in front of him. "You've changed."

He laid his head back on his arms. "I guess."

The door crashed suddenly back on its hinges into the wall.

"You're gonna get it, you're gonna get it!" Stevie chanted, clearly delighted.

"Shut up, creepazoid!" Diana shouted.

Stevie stuck his tongue out at her, then turned back to him. "We're *never* supposed to leave without telling someone. You're gonna get it!"

Cameron felt a jolt of fear run through him. Maybe it would be more than twenty strokes.

"Beat it, Stevie!" Diana told him. "I'm warning you—"

"It's my room," Stevie retorted. "And I didn't go anywhere. I stayed around the house like I was supposed to. I'm not in trouble like you—"

"That's it!" Diana shouted, rising up from her cross-legged position in fury. "You get away with murder going off on your own, you little jerk!"

"Stop it!" Cameron heard his voice overpower Diana's.

They both looked at him.

"Stevie's right," Cameron said more quietly. "We broke a rule, and we're in trouble. Fighting about how much trouble isn't going to make it any better."

Stevie looked startled.

Cameron sighed and laid his head back on his arms. "Just leave me alone, will you?"

Diana studied him thoughtfully. Then she took Stevie's arm and turned him toward the door, and the two of them went out of the room without another word.

Cameron sat there as the afternoon wore on, listening to the geese honking as they flew over the lake and wondering how bad the punishment would be. He'd figured out that thanks to Neil's going off alone six years ago, this was the worst rule he could have broken. He wanted the Laceys to love him the way they had loved Neil, and he knew he deserved this punishment, but—

Pop had been right, he thought in despair. Cameron could never be good enough to make up for how bad he'd been. Through all the soul-crushing nights and the aspirin-popping days, he'd survived because he'd gone on hoping. He'd promised himself that if he took his punishment, if he tried to be good, something would happen. He wasn't quite sure what, but the pain would be over at last, and he'd be glad he'd hung on.

The hum of the air-conditioning filled the room, and he felt cold in his corner. His right leg ached where Pop had broken the bone two summers ago and set it himself, cursing Cameron for the extra trouble. There were a lot of aches when he got chilled, but that one was the worst. He wished he were out on the lake in the Sunfish, with the hot sun beating down on him and the golden highlights of the water shimmering into his eyes. He had loved the sailing every bit as much as he'd dreamed he would. Even with Diana's eyes jealously following him, even knowing that her boat was only a few lengths behind his, Cameron had felt free. He'd thought his endurance had finally paid off.

Why did you do it, Neil? He couldn't understand why a boy who had parents and a home and a sailboat had broken a rule like that and gone off alone. *And why did you go with Hank Miller?* At least Neil's father wouldn't kill him, he thought. He wasn't like Pop in that respect— or in certain others, Cameron had begun to believe. But the punishment he'd earned would still be severe. Wasn't there any other way to express a parent's love? Only if a kid could be good enough, he guessed.

He shut his eyes and remembered the breeze rushing into his face, blinding him mercifully, the flapping of the sail as he came about, the magic of running with the wind. He thought he'd found freedom at last, but it was only an illusion of escape. Cameron felt hope die slowly in his heart. He would never be done paying for how bad he'd been.

11

Punishment

"Neil?"

He jumped, his stomach lurching. He hadn't realized how late it had gotten. He looked up fearfully and saw Neil's father standing over him. The man had on his suit from work, not the jeans he'd worn around the house over the weekend, and he looked cold and forbidding. Cameron got to his feet quickly, his legs cottony and tingling from being doubled up for so long, and the broken bone aching worse than ever.

"I'm sorry," he said quickly. "I didn't think, but it was still my fault, not Diana's. I should be the one who gets punished."

His father unbuttoned his suit jacket and sat down on Neil's bed. He sighed and loosened his necktie, then unbuttoned his collar button before sliding the tie off. Cameron stared at the necktie, feeling a cold sweat pop out on his back. Would the man tie his hands to the post of the headboard before beating him? Perhaps he should have stayed on the floor instead of standing up before being ordered to.

"I'm sorry," he repeated dully.

"Your mother was very worried," his father said in the neutral tone of voice that Cameron recognized from the hospital. "She came into the kitchen and found you missing again, and it was a great shock for her. Can you understand that?"

Cameron nodded, watching the strong hands smooth and fold the tie. "Yes, sir."

The man frowned, and Cameron wondered if calling him "sir" had been a mistake. Sometimes Pop had liked it, but other times he'd thought it was back talk.

"Look, Neil—you've been through a lot, but we have, too. I wanted you to settle in and feel comfortable being back home before starting therapy, but maybe I was wrong. Maybe we need some family therapy to start working together again." He sighed. "Try to think what it's been like for us—worrying about you, thinking you were gone for good, then finding you again. Can you imagine that at all?"

Cameron nodded again. "Yes," he whispered. Why couldn't the man just get on with it? Where was the belt, anyway? Surely he wasn't going to use that thin suit belt he was wearing. Then Cameron remembered fearing that it might be worse than a belt. He knew there were wooden clothes hangers in Stevie's closet, and he felt the room close in around him until he could barely breathe.

The hazel eyes looked squarely at him. "Yes, I think you can imagine it. I think you've grown up a lot." The eyes looked away suddenly, darkening painfully. "I'm sorry that growing up cost you so much." The man swallowed, then straightened his shoulders. "But I want you to make something out of the suffering. I want you to think more about what effect your actions are going to have on the people around you. Can you understand that?"

Cameron nodded, unable to speak because of the fear pulsing through him. His back throbbed as though the wooden dowel of the hanger had already slammed over it. Neil's father stood up, and Cameron's heart turned over as the tie slid through the man's fingers.

"Okay," his father said. "That means telling Mrs. Pierson or your mother or me if you go somewhere, and being back by the time you promise. Now come on down to supper."

Cameron stared stupidly, a sense of loss flooding over him. His father must have realized that he wasn't following, because he turned back to look at him quizzically.

"What?"

Cameron swallowed. "What about my punishment?" he made himself ask, his voice cracking.

His father smiled at him. "What—you think I should ground you? I think you've punished yourself enough worrying about it, haven't you? It's all right, Neil. I know you didn't mean to frighten us. In the future, just *think*, okay?"

Cameron felt light-headed. He didn't know whether to believe the man, or to wait for punishment to come in the dark. But the man had only stood there the other nights—surely he wouldn't—with Stevie there— Cameron shook his head, trying to think straight. These past nights he'd seen that there was nothing to fear in the dark. No one did anything in this house at night except sleep and watch over one another. He didn't have to fear a worse punishment after everyone had gone to bed.

He followed the man out of the room shakily, his legs trembling. The part of him that felt relief was soaring, but a deeper part of him felt lost. Didn't they care enough about him to punish him? Suddenly, fervently, he wished Pop were there, to shake his head and raise the belt, and offer hope that someday, if Cameron took his punishment, he would learn how to be good.

He saw Neil's father head into his bedroom and toss his tie on the bedspread, followed by his suit jacket. *He only took the tie off because he was finally home and he'd had it on all day*, Cameron realized. Neil's father wasn't anything like Pop at all. The man sat on the bed and looked up at him through those eerily familiar hazel eyes as he untied his shoelaces.

"Go on, tell your mother you won't give her a scare like that again," he said, grinning. Then the grin faded. "Are you all right, Neil?"

He swallowed and tried to say, "Yes."

His father frowned at him and dropped the shoe he was holding. "What is it?"

Cameron shook his head helplessly. He had been prepared to deal with the beating, but he had no idea how to take the reprieve. "I thought—I thought you'd..." He didn't want to say *beat me,* because he didn't think that was what ordinary people in nice homes like this did to their kids. What could he say? "...spank me," he finished lamely.

"'Spank you'?" his father repeated, disbelieving.

Cameron nodded. "He—Hank—he would have," he tried to explain. "With a belt," he went on when his father said nothing. "Or a strap. Or something." He swallowed and stared at the lone shoe lying on its side on the beige carpet, trying not to think about wooden hangers. "To teach me how to be good," he said, groping for words, "because he—loved me. He said."

"That son of a—" Neil's father reached out to him, and Cameron flinched before he could stop himself.

His father took a deep breath and let it out explosively. "Neil, Hank Miller is dead. He'll never touch you again, and no one else will ever do what he did to you. I will never take a belt or a strap or anything else to you, no matter what you do wrong. That isn't a sign of love, that's—that's violence. That's wrong. Believe me. I may ground you, I may give you extra chores, I may forbid you to ride your bike or watch television, but I will never punish you by physically hurting you. Never."

Cameron looked up at him. The voice sounded as though the man himself was hurting, and Cameron saw that his father's face was drawn in pain. "I-I'm sorry," he stammered. "I didn't mean—"

"I thought I knew what it must have been like," his father said in a low voice. "I thought I'd come to terms with what he'd done to you. I guess I've got a ways to go." He met Cameron's eyes and managed a smile. "We'll get there, son. Just trust me—I won't hurt you. Now go on out to your mom."

Cameron nodded and turned away, toward the living room. He knew he should feel relieved, but he felt adrift. This man was good. He would never understand how bad Cameron was, letting all those boys die because he couldn't make them understand—letting Neil die. Cameron slowly started down the hall, his guilt as vivid for him as the memory of the cellar's sickly sweet smell. He could never be punished enough to be forgiven. Why had he ever hoped?

"Oh," his father's voice followed him, stronger now, trying to change the subject. "Tell her that when I get there I'll fill you all in on the latest in the police I.D. saga—that Detective Simmons was not very pleased about your dental charts, to put it mildly."

The guilt turned to tension again. What was wrong with the dental charts? But his father didn't sound worried, more amused. Could Detective Simmons take him away even if the Laceys believed he was Neil? Slowly, Cameron made his way to the living room to apologize again to his mother. She hugged him tightly for a long moment, then finally released him and wiped her eyes, smiling unsteadily at him. He looked away, confused because part of him had actually liked her embrace, and eased himself down cross-legged on the floor near the plate-glass window, where he could see the lake. He tried not to notice Diana looking at him curiously.

When his father reappeared, he looked a good deal less threatening in jeans and a plaid flannel shirt with the sleeves rolled up, and he was smiling as if the previous conversation had not occurred. Cameron realized that it would stay just between the two of them. His mother handed his father a drink, and he gave her a quick hug before taking a long swallow and dropping down into an armchair. He grinned at Cameron.

"You've got good teeth, Neil."

Cameron realized that this must have something to do with the dental charts, but he wasn't sure what it meant. He looked away and watched Stevie wander in and sit on the floor next to his father's chair.

"So?" Diana asked. She was standing in the doorway between the dining room and the living room, leaning against the wall. "Is that supposed to prove he's Neil or something?"

"Diana!" Her mother looked furious.

"Pipe down, Diana," her father said, keeping his smile in place. "We *know* he's Neil. It's only Detective Simmons who doesn't."

"What do you mean?" Cameron asked, nervous.

"Well," his father explained, sounding like the lawyer he was, the way he had in the hospital, "Detective Simmons has raised quite a stink. He's told the other members of the task force, the doctors, anyone who'll listen, that he doesn't believe in happy endings. So—since he feels compelled to make a positive identification, I was hoping to match up your dental records. You see, before you disappeared you used to go to the dentist regularly, and he has charts of your mouth that show cavities and fillings. If they match the charts of your mouth today, then you're the same kid, right?"

Cameron nodded uncertainly.

"Wrong," his father said. "Because you *are* a kid. When you disappeared you still had a lot of baby teeth, and those have since come out and been replaced by permanent teeth."

"But he had some of his permanent teeth by then," his mother said.

His father nodded. "That's where the problem of the good teeth comes in. You see, Neil didn't have any cavities or fillings in his permanent teeth at his last checkup before he disappeared. He's got some cavities now, but that's a normal part of growing up. If they could definitely match a filling from before with a filling there now, then that would be a positive identification that Detective Simmons would have to accept. Or if they could find an old filling that had magically disappeared, then Detective Simmons could claim that he's not Neil. Unfortunately, there's no proof either way. As far as the suspicious Detective Simmons is concerned"—his father smiled, trying to make it into a joke—"that's not conclusive."

Cameron remembered the hatred in the detective's

voice that day in the hospital when they'd thought he was unconscious, and the way he'd been waiting outside the emergency room entrance when the Laceys took Cameron home. Detective Simmons didn't believe he was Neil and was determined to prove it.

"Is there any way to convince that man?" his mother asked, rubbing her arms as though she were cold. "What about DNA testing?"

His father sighed. "Well, Simmons mentioned that, but I'm not sure *what* will persuade him. Now he says it's a matter for forensics. They're still analyzing the bodies and linking them to the missing boys. If there's one left over, and if somehow the forensic pathologist can make a positive match with Neil, Simmons could claim that's conclusive. Conversely, if the bodies are all identified as other boys, then Simmons will have to admit that Neil is Neil."

"Can he take me away?" Cameron asked, his voice shaking slightly. Between the mention of forensics and the question about DNA testing, he didn't know what to think.

"Of course not," his mother said quickly.

"Not without a lot more evidence than he has now," his father said more slowly. "Don't you worry about it, Neil. This time anyone who wants you has to go through me."

"What *about* the DNA testing?" Diana asked suddenly. Cameron looked at her.

"That's not the issue here," her father said evenly.

"But—" Diana started. Then she met her father's

eyes and looked away. "Well then, what about the bodies? How long will it take to identify them?"

"Please, Diana—" her mother said. "Don't be morbid."

"But what if he's not Neil?" the girl asked.

"Diana!" Her mother whirled on her and slapped her, hard, then burst into tears. In one swift movement, Neil's father was up from the chair and across the room to his wife. "She didn't mean anything, Annie," he said softly. "Of course he's Neil."

Stevie looked over curiously, and Cameron looked away.

"I'm sorry," his mother whispered, wiping her cheeks. "I'm so sorry, Diana." She took a slow, shuddering breath. "All right, then—how long will it take to identify the—the bodies?"

"This is very high priority," his father assured her, keeping one arm around her shoulders. "They want to be able to tell the other families for certain what happened to their sons. Simmons seems to think the pathologist should have answers in a week or so. Twenty-three bodies—that's a lot of work."

Diana lowered her hand from her reddening cheek and glared at her parents, then turned to Cameron, but he barely noticed her reflection in the plate-glass window. As he stared at the lake, the setting sun dipped on the horizon and the water beneath it swirled blood red.

He had read twenty-two files in Hank Miller's cellar. The police had to have found the file cabinet—they'd know the boys went with the files. Pop couldn't have started a file on the last boy yet, Josh, because there hadn't been any news stories about his disappearance before the police had surrounded Miller's house. Twenty-three bodies, including Josh's, meant that forensics would match one body to every file, including the remains of Neil Lacey.

12

The Stalker

Cameron strode along the downtown sidewalk the next Monday morning, feeling guilty. The Laceys had thought he was upset because the talk of the bodies must have reminded him of the things Hank Miller had done to him, and they'd spent all weekend fussing over him. Except for Diana and Stevie, of course. His mother had asked Mrs. Pierson to make fried chicken for Friday night's dinner—Neil's favorite. Stevie had sulked, pulling the skin off his fried chicken distastefully and crunching the bones, oblivious to his mother's glare. Diana had just sat there staring at Cameron thoughtfully and eating little. She'd gone sailing with him on Friday, but had spoken to him as little as possible. She just kept looking at him, as if she were studying a particularly obnoxious but nonetheless fascinating insect.

Somehow their parents had managed to make a nice family dinner out of the fried chicken in the end. His mother had gotten Stevie talking about his latest computer game, and the little kid finally cracked a smile at her, lighting up his whole face. Then their father had asked Diana about the books she'd gotten at the library, and he discussed some of them with her, sounding like he actually valued what she thought. Pop had never wanted to know what Cameron was thinking. He listened to them discussing the *Dark Is Rising* books, which he'd already read. Diana was saying it was unfair in the books that Will Stanton ended up being distanced from his family because of his powers as an Old One.

"It's unfair," Cameron heard himself saying before he could stop to think, "but it's honest." He shut up, wishing he hadn't spoken. Now Diana would turn to him with that flat look of dislike, and the warm atmosphere of the family meal would die. He'd enjoyed sitting there, watching them, almost feeling a part of them.

To his surprise, Diana and her father both looked at him with interest. "How can it be both unfair and honest?" the man asked, and Diana looked like she wanted to know the answer, too.

"It's also unfair that Bran's dog is killed," Cameron explained slowly. "It's unfair that John Rowlands's wife, who's been so beautiful and so loving, turns out to be so evil. But I think it's honest because the point is that you have to pay a price when the Light stands against the Dark. It seems unfair in regular, everyday life, but it's the price you pay to do the right thing."

Diana studied him for a moment. Then she said, thoughtfully, "I see what you mean. It's unfair if you only look at it and see the here and now. But if you look at it through the eyes of an Old One, who sees all time, it is fair. A heavy price, but a fair price."

Cameron nodded, and nearly blushed when she smiled at him. She almost looked like she approved of him, the way she'd approve of a real brother.

He'd been surprised by how much he liked feeling part of the Lacey family. He'd only hoped to feel safe, and to sail free at last, but he seemed to be on the verge of finding something more—something worth the effort of questioning every action, every moment, always asking, *Would Neil do that?* Being part of a real family, belonging somewhere at last—that would be worth it. Pop certainly wasn't like the families he'd read about in books and imagined. The Laceys weren't, either, with prickly Diana and sulky Stevie, but he'd liked sitting there at the supper table, surrounded by their voices and laughter. He'd liked cooking out with them Saturday, using an air gun to blow on the coals to keep the fire hot, and shooting the air at Stevie, making the little kid laugh. He'd liked going to church with them on Sunday, even with the other people in the congregation staring at him.

And he'd liked seeing the parents holding hands in the evenings, while the family watched television after dinner. He wanted to be a part of that family. If only he could work out what Neil's father had meant about love and punishment. The rules of sailing were clear enough, but the other rules were hazy here, not like Pop's clear-cut punishments and the hope that got Cameron through them. Now he wasn't sure how he'd ever learn to be good. The only punishments he could imagine were what Detective Simmons would do to him when he identified the bodies, and what Cougar would do to him if he found him.

In spite of the peaceful days, Cameron had lain awake in the dark each night, listening to Stevie's even breathing and remembering the nights from his past, and the angry, heavy-fisted young man Pop had nicknamed Cougar. He had been headstrong and short-tempered, not careful like Pop. Look how quickly he got arrested on his own. Maybe it had something to do with the way his own pop had treated him when he was a kid. And the time in prison would probably have turned him meaner.

Cameron had still been awake Sunday night when he heard the floor creak and realized that his father had come in to check on him again. He surprised himself by sliding into sleep while the man still stood at the foot of his bed, and not waking until Cougar strode into his dreams, his fist snapping sharply into Cameron's cheekbone, sending flashing pain into his eye and jerking him upright in bed.

He was relieved that both his parents were dressed for work Monday morning at breakfast. He needed some time to think. They'd never discussed the newspaper article last week, and he needed to decide whether he should talk to the Laceys about Cougar.

His mother didn't seem wholly comfortable with the idea of leaving him alone, though. "I could stay home today, Neil—I don't have to go into work this week—I could take some more vacation time." She put down the piece of toast she was buttering and frowned at him, troubled.

Stevie rolled his eyes and spooned more sugar on his cereal, but neither of his parents noticed.

His father reached over and squeezed his mother's hand. "Come on, now, Annie. You know we discussed this. I think we need to get back to our regular routine, and give Neil a chance to relax and settle in."

"I know," she said slowly. "Neil, are you sure that's all right with you?"

He nodded. "Sure," he said, and quickly added, "Mom." That didn't seem to be enough, so he said, "I'll be fine. Really."

She had finally left for work, reluctantly, hugging him at the garage doorway as if she couldn't bear to let him go. Something inside Cameron had surprised him by not wanting her to release him, either.

Now, as he strode along the sidewalk, he put his head down and walked faster. Cougar would want to get even with Pop, and with Hank Miller dead Cameron was afraid Cougar would look for Hank's son. What would the man do when he heard that Hank's son had turned out to be Neil Lacey?

He wished he could remember how long Cougar had

known Pop. It was one of those things that seemed to have no beginning in his memory, like dreaming of sailing, or wondering what had happened to his mother. If Cougar hadn't met up with Pop until after Neil's murder, then he might believe Cameron really was Neil Lacey. Would he come after him then, or would he leave him alone?

But if Cougar had been with Pop when Neil was killed, then he'd know that Cameron was lying. How long would it take him to find the Laceys? Cameron wondered if he could get his father to go to the police and ask them for protection. But the police weren't on his side. If Cougar turned up and said that Cameron wasn't Neil after all, Detective Simmons would have his positive identification. He'd jerk Cameron out of the Lacey household so fast— *At least that would make Diana and Stevie happy,* Cameron thought bitterly.

"Need a lift?"

He'd been so absorbed in his thoughts, Cameron hadn't heard the car pull up beside him. He jumped back, and then recognized the sleek silver-gray and blue of the police car. Detective Simmons smiled thinly at him through the open passenger window.

"You shouldn't be out alone," he said. "You might disappear again."

Cameron wiped his palms on his jeans. "I told Mrs. Pierson where I was going," he stammered. "I just needed some time alone."

The detective nodded. "Time to think, hmm? Time to plan your next move?"

"No—"

"Better think fast," Simmons said, his voice hardening. "The labs are going to have proof that Neil Lacey is dead by the end of the week. They're moving fast."

Cameron shook his head wordlessly, backing away. This detective was just like Pop—the best thing to do was keep quiet.

"You think you're so clever," Simmons said, his voice thick with disgust. "Worming your way into their family—preying on their love of their son." He made his voice high and boyish. "'Oooh, Mama Bear, don't cry!'" Cameron flinched, and the detective went on, "I was in the hallway in the hospital—I heard you playing her like a master. She gave an interview about her little boy calling her Mama Bear—did you see it on television, or did you read about it? It was in the newspaper, and in more than one magazine."

Cameron flushed with shame and was sure the detective could see it in his face. *He knows about the clippings— he knows how I've done it.* Even worse was the thought that if the detective knew, the Laceys would find out. It would hurt them terribly, maybe even worse than losing Neil the first time. When they sent him to prison, Cameron would have to add that guilt to his guilt over the boys.

"Or did Neil tell you himself?" The detective's gaze bored into him, relentless. "What was it like, Cameron, knowing the boys? Making friends with them? Then watching him torture them? Did you like it, the way your father did?"

"No!" Cameron cried, his voice thin and high, horror making him forget caution. "No! I didn't—"

"Didn't what?" the detective interrupted. "No, you didn't make friends with them? No, you didn't watch? —Did you help your father, instead?"

"Stop it!" Cameron cried. He wanted to run, but he was too frightened. The detective would put on the siren— he'd chase him down—he'd arrest him. And then he'd tell the Laceys everything, and Cameron would see the love they felt for Neil turn into hatred for him.

"I've been working on my own time," Simmons told him. "I've found witnesses who remember Hank Miller's little boy from before Neil disappeared. How is that possible, do you think?"

"I don't know!" stammered Cameron helplessly. "I'll tell my father you stopped me today."

"You do that," the detective said. "Tell Neil Lacey's father—the man you're deceiving. I'll tell him I was keeping an eye on you, making sure that nothing else happened to you. After all, you've been through a lot."

"I'll tell him what you said," Cameron said, but his voice faltered. Arguing always made it worse in the end.

"Will you?" Detective Simmons smiled. "I'll be very surprised if you do."

When Cameron said nothing, the detective's smile widened and he nodded his head slowly. "Look, I think the walls are closing in around you," Simmons said. He sounded like Pop, explaining why he had to do something he didn't want to. He reached toward his jacket, which had been flung across the passenger's seat, and

Cameron nearly found himself extending his wrists for the handcuffs, already feeling the cool steel encircling them. Pop used handcuffs sometimes, though not too often on him. He used them on the boys in the end, when it was clear they were beyond hope.

Instead Simmons pulled a business card from his jacket pocket and held it out the window. "Here, take this. When the walls get too close, give me a call and tell me the truth about who you really are." Then his smile faded. "Go on, take it. But don't wait too long. After the labs prove you're Cameron Miller, I'll come arrest you whether you call or not. And there's nothing that lawyer will be able to do about it."

Silently Cameron took the business card, his hand damp and shaking. The detective gunned his motor and drove off.

Cameron watched the car for a few moments, then slipped the business card into his hip pocket without looking at it. He turned and stumbled back the way he'd come, on weak, trembling legs. He was supposed to meet Diana at the Burger Biggie in half an hour, and he could go straight there now. He'd be safe in the bright lights, with the plastic tables crowded with other teenagers around him, laughing and talking. But thinking about the smell of french fries and greasy burgers turned his stomach. Anyway, he'd wanted to be alone for a while.

He used to have more time alone than he knew what to do with. Then he'd hidden in dreams of sailing to blank out the emptiness. Now he was feeling almost smothered by the Laceys' attention, and he needed time to think, not to blank out. Something was nagging at the edge of his mind, but he couldn't quite bring it into focus—something wrong with what Neil's father had said about punishment, something that was important. But it dissolved into images of Pop when he got too close to it.

He turned down a deserted side street and walked on, staring at his feet again. Was there anything he could do about Detective Simmons? That business about having proof that Pop had a kid before Neil disappeared—that was bad. It had been crazy for him not to have thought of it. Just because he couldn't remember most of his past didn't mean that other people wouldn't remember seeing him. He should have thought...

Maybe he should just disappear again. But he wasn't even fifteen yet. How could he live? The thought of running away, ending up in a bus station, hungry, going home in the end with someone else like Pop—it was more than he could face. A couple of the boys had said that Pop had picked them up in the Knoxville bus station.

And Neil's father hadn't mentioned this new objection. Pop kept so alone, maybe people really hadn't seen Cameron before he started school. Maybe Simmons was lying, trying to trap him.

Cameron was beginning to feel better when he walked straight into a man. Before he could open his mouth to apologize, the man's hand shot out and grabbed a handful of his T-shirt and slammed him around into the windowless concrete wall of a warehouse.

"I've been waiting for you, Cameron," Cougar said, grinning that crazy mean grin. "As soon as they let me out I asked myself, *Now, what could have happened to Hank's little boy?* I figured he'd want me to look after you, don't you think?"

There seemed to be no air in the shadowy side street, only the weight of Cougar's fist pressing in on his chest.

"I gotta admit it," Cougar went on. "A town like Freeport—a family like the Laceys—I'm impressed. You're on to a good thing, kid. You're smart, like your pop."

Cameron drew in a great gasp of air and let it out in jerks. The man looked just as he remembered, with shifty, ink-black eyes and slicked-back black hair. But he had an edge on him that he hadn't had before, a hardening of the line of his jaw. He'd lost weight, too, and there was a puckered scar running down the left side of his face and neck that Cameron didn't remember.

"Smart," Cougar said, slapping Cameron's cheek so sharply his head rocked back against the rough concrete of the wall. "You should have gone to reform school for accessory, you know that? Instead here you are, rich family, welcomed home by grateful Mommy and Daddy." He laughed shortly. "Of course, they don't know you very well, do they? I wonder how grateful they'd be if they knew they had Hank Miller's little boy instead of their own."

The tension returned, and Cameron kept quiet, the way he had with Pop. Cougar laughed again.

"Question is, who'd be more grateful? Mommy and Daddy if I tell them who you really are? Grateful enough to pay, anyway? Or you?" His voice hardened, and he shook Cameron and forced him to meet his eyes. "How grateful would you be if I kept your little secret?"

"I don't have any money," Cameron whispered.

Cougar shook him hard. "You learned to lie from your pop, too, didn't you? He was a great liar, setting me up like that. And you lied for him. So don't lie to me now, Cameron Miller. The Laceys have money—do you give it to me, or do I blow your story and get it from Mommy and Daddy?"

"Please—"

Cougar slammed him against the wall again, and the coarse texture of the concrete scraped his back through the thin cotton of his T-shirt. "Empty your pockets."

Cameron fumbled in his jeans, remembering what he'd read in the newspaper about how Cougar had been abused as a kid. Somewhere inside of the man there had to be something he could reach—Cougar was just like him. He had to be.

Cameron's hand closed around the ten-dollar bill his father had given him for his allowance, and he held out the money. "It's all I've got," he said. "Really."

Cougar snatched it, frowning. "Then get more, boy. You hear me? A couple days—I'll meet you here Thursday, and you have some real money for me, or something I can sell easy, like jewelry nobody's blown the whistle on yet, right? You show me how grateful you are for me keeping my mouth shut, or I'll find out how grateful Mommy and Daddy can be."

Cameron stumbled backward as the man's fist opened and released his shirt. "I know what happened to you," he made himself say. "I know what your own pop did to you, like Pop did to me. But it's over now, Cougar—"

"Don't call me that!" the man screamed. His black eyes widened and flicked rapidly from side to side, looking up and down the street. A muscle in his cheek twitched.

He looks afraid, Cameron thought.

Then Cougar shoved him hard in the chest. "And you don't know nothing, boy. Just forget I ever had a pop, got it? You and me—we're nothing alike. You, you're a mouse in a trap. Me, I'm the cat that's going to get you."

Then he got himself under control, and his lips stretched into that crazy mean grin. "But we're partners now, aren't we? Cat and mouse partners. So I'll make you a deal. You don't call me Cougar, I don't call you Cameron. I'm Bill Scott, okay? Deal, Neil?"

He waved two fingers in a snappy salute and walked down the narrow street, laughing at his rhyme. "Thursday!" he called over his shoulder.

Cameron straightened his T-shirt with nerveless fingers and rubbed his stinging cheek. In the newspaper the lawyer had said that Cougar needed therapy. If he'd gotten any in prison, it certainly hadn't changed him. Cougar was just the same. Cameron leaned against the cool concrete wall, wanting to blank out the meeting, but afraid to. What would Cougar—Scott—do?

Maybe it would be better to tell the Laceys right now, or call Simmons and tell him his hunch was right after all. Then he realized that it wouldn't do any good to go to the police and admit he wasn't Neil. The cops would just arrest him. Who cared if a man who'd been falsely convicted threatened the serial murderer's lying son who'd helped put him behind bars?

But Cougar wanted a payback for the time he'd spent in prison. He thought the Laceys were rich. Even if Simmons took Cameron away, Cougar might decide to take enough from the Laceys to make up for the lost blackmail opportunity, and Cameron couldn't let him loose on the family who'd taken him in. Somehow he had to get hold of enough money to pay off Cougar for good.

The asphalt blurred before his eyes, and he blinked at hot tears. Cougar was wrong. The two of them *were* just alike. Did that mean he'd grow up to be like Cougar, hurting kids because he had been hurt? If that was true, why bother?

13

Vote of No Confidence

"What are you doing here?"

Cameron looked up at Diana from where he sat cross-legged on the rough redwood planks at the edge of the dock on Tuesday morning. "Waiting for you," he said, squinting into the sun, "to go sailing."

She sighed exaggeratedly and sat down behind him, propping herself against the dock railing. He had to pivot around to face her, scratching the crossed sides of his legs slightly on the splintery edges of the boards.

"That's not what I mean," she said. "Look—you're not my brother Neil. I don't know who you are, but I want to know what you're doing here. What do you want from my family?"

This time the question didn't surprise him. He remembered how she'd made the suggestion on Thursday night, and how her mother had slapped her. Friday night, she'd been nice to him about the books. And she'd been polite over the weekend, too. But she hadn't been too pleased about having to pay for his burger at lunch the day before, though he'd been too shaken from meeting Cougar to spare much thought for her. Now her expression was remote. Diana looked almost exactly the way her father had looked the day he faced down the doctor at the hospital.

Should he just confess? Give up and turn himself in to Detective Simmons, and escape Cougar once and for all? But that would mean leaving the Lacey family exposed to Cougar's anger. And it would also mean giving up on himself, and his chance to stay with a family who could love him. Cameron couldn't bring himself to do that yet.

"You're losing it," he said shortly. "Of course I'm Neil."

"Give me a break. Neil was a bully and a jerk. He pushed me and Stevie around all the time. You're not anything like him. Neil wouldn't have played with Stevie while we were cooking out. He never liked fantasy like the *Dark Is Rising* books, and he wouldn't have cared about the price of doing the right thing even if he *had* read them. He'd never have taken the blame for going to the library—he would have told Mom it was all my fault, and he would have grabbed that amnesia excuse and said he didn't remember the rule. He would have weaseled out of it and left me to take the rap."

Diana looked away at the lake. "They'd have grounded me, you know," she added after a moment. "They always let Neil off."

"You want me to be more of a jerk?" he asked roughly. "Well, forget it. I've seen enough bullying. I'm not the same."

"Definitely not," she said, smiling a little. "So, if you're not Neil, who are you? And what's your angle?"

"I'm Neil," he said flatly. "And I don't have any angle. Right now I just want to go sailing."

"Well, you *are* like Neil in that respect," she conceded. "He always wanted to be out on the water, away from everybody." Then her voice sharpened. "But if you really were Neil you wouldn't have waited for me today. You'd have cast off, and if Mom or Dad or Mrs. Pierson caught you, you'd have told them that I promised I'd be there and then didn't show, and they'd have blamed me—"

"Come off it," Cameron said, taken aback by her bitterness. "You've built me into some kind of monster in your mind. You said you wanted to be an actress— maybe you like blowing everything up into some great drama you can star in. I wasn't that bad."

"Neil was worse," she said flatly. "He told lies, and he blackmailed me and Stevie if we didn't back him up. He took things at school, and from us—and even from Mom and Dad. And they always believed *him*! Neil's the one who was such a great actor. Grown-ups always believed every story he told them."

Cameron turned away, wincing inside. If Neil was anything like she said, maybe he deserved the punishment Pop had given him, after all. But no kid deserved that. . . .

And wasn't he just as bad as Neil? He was acting,

lying to the Laceys and to everybody. While he'd been sitting on the dock waiting for Diana, he'd been trying to figure out what he could take to pay off Cougar. He was as much of a thief as Neil, even if he was stealing to get rid of Cougar. After all, he'd already stolen Neil's future; and, if he was going to be honest with himself, he had to admit that the Laceys' money mattered to him. He wasn't sure that he'd have picked Neil if his family hadn't been so well off. He was worse than Neil—he was as bad as Cougar.

"I'm sorry," he said finally.

"Don't be," she told him. "It's not your fault, because you're not Neil. And I don't care about that—I'd rather have you for a brother than him, anyway. I like you—I can't imagine ever liking Neil. What I want to know is what you're doing here."

"Trying to forget," he said bitterly. "Trying to get back to life—trying to survive."

"Stop lying!" Diana snapped. "Stop pretending to be like Neil! Everything you do—you're pretending, and I can see it!" She was practically screaming at him, her voice hard and angry like Pop's. "Neil was always on the move, lots of nervous energy, talking with his hands and bouncing around, and you're so still and quiet!"

Pop liked him still and quiet. Cameron could remember Pop slapping his hands, then finally tying them and leaving them tied, to keep him from using them. Not handcuffs, though—Pop saved the handcuffs for special times, mostly for the boys at the very end. Pop had tied Cameron's hands with thick twine that felt scratchy at first, and then dug into his wrists until they bled. When

Pop untied him at last, Cameron was so grateful he didn't want to move his hands anymore. But how could he put that into words that Diana would understand?

The girl was almost shouting, "You don't like the foods Neil liked, you don't read the kind of books he liked, you don't even remember any of Neil's jokes! You're *not* my brother! Admit it! Who are you? Tell me!"

He remembered Pop's orders. *You tell me the truth, boy—you come right out with it and admit what you've done and take your punishment. If I ever find out you failed to admit the truth to me . . .* And Pop would glance meaningfully at the cellar. Diana sounded just like him. She'd lost that dispassionate expression that made her look so like her father, and now she looked like Pop—angry, unforgiving. She looked murderous.

Cameron's mouth opened. Part of him screamed, *Admit who you really are and take your punishment!* But part of him whispered, *She doesn't know anything—she's just hurt, and angry. Don't do anything. Just keep quiet.* He knew that voice all too well. It was the voice that had always kept him silent as Pop got more and more impatient with the boys. It was the voice that kept him silent when Pop said he had to teach them a lesson, once and for all. It was the voice that kept him silent when the police came to question him about Cougar. *Just keep quiet. Survive. And don't think about what it costs anyone else.*

He closed his mouth. He took a deep breath. Then he said, "I'm Neil Lacey. I *am* your brother."

"You're not!" she exploded. "Even the way you're sitting! Neil hated sitting cross-legged. He said it was a stupid way to sit. He used to get in so much trouble from teachers in assemblies. I always did it right, but I could hear Neil's teacher scolding him about it."

Cameron remembered Pop ordering him to sit cross-legged on the floor to listen to him, or to watch television. It wasn't the most comfortable way to sit, and after a while his knees always hurt, but Pop beat him if he moved. He stared at Diana, thinking that if the teachers had beaten Neil instead of scolding him, the kid might have shut up and sat still. But all he said was, "People change. You don't expect me to still do every dumb thing I did when I was eight, do you?" He was relieved that his voice sounded steadier than he felt.

"Of course not," she said. "I don't expect you to pick your nose, or make gross armpit squeaks, or even watch stupid cartoons. But some habits you don't break."

He straightened his legs and stood up. "All habits can be broken," he told her. "It just takes enough punishment." But he wondered again how many little things he'd slipped up on that he didn't even realize yet. When his father studied him, was that what he was thinking? *Neil always did this or that—why don't you?* How many allowances would the Laceys make for him before they stopped believing he was their son, and started believing Detective Simmons?

Cameron swung down from the dock into his Sunfish, not caring whether Diana followed him in hers. He just wanted to be on the lake while he still could, while the adult Laceys, at least, still believed him. And maybe Diana had actually helped him—if he was going to be

Neil, he might as well act more like him. Apparently, if you didn't live with Pop you didn't have to obey the rules all the time.

"Hey," she said suddenly. "What happened to your face?"

The bruise was starting to darken where Cougar had struck him, though it wasn't very bad. *Stupid*, Cameron thought. Pop never hit him where it showed, only where his clothes hid the bruises and scars. But Cougar wasn't smart enough for that.

"I fell off Stevie's bike," he told her. "I threw out my hand, but I was too near the curb and it smacked me on the cheek. No big deal."

"I don't believe you," she said slowly. "Are you in some kind of trouble?"

"So what else is new?" Cameron retorted. "You don't believe me about anything." He released the mooring line.

"What are you going to do?" he challenged her as he pushed away from the dock. "Tell Dad I went sailing alone? Tell him you think I'm lying? Tell him you don't believe I'm Neil? Because he believes me!"

"Sure he does!" she shouted after him. She stood up and hurried to her own boat. "He always believed Neil—he loved Neil, and he never cared about me or Stevie. And now he loves you, whoever you are." She dropped into her boat and cast off before he was ten feet from the dock. "And if I don't go sailing with you, it's not *you* who'll get in trouble, anyway—it's me!"

"Don't worry," he told her. "I wouldn't get you in

trouble. I don't care if you believe me or not, but I don't ever want to see anybody punished for me."

Cameron turned his back on her and hoisted his sail, careful to cleat the halyard securely. Then he dropped the daggerboard and hauled in the mainsheet so that the sail caught the wind and filled out. He grabbed the tiller and turned the bow away until he was almost running downwind.

The air rushed past him as the boat picked up speed, roaring in his ears to drown out Diana's words. Cameron didn't care if she was behind him or not. He didn't care if she got out of her boat and went back in the house. He didn't care if she blamed him for sailing alone. He didn't even care if Neil's father had another talk with him about breaking rules.

He felt free. Out here on the lake, Diana couldn't remind him that he was a liar and a thief. Cougar couldn't touch him. He doubted that Cougar could even sail, and felt a surge of relief that they really were different in some ways. Then he gave himself over to the Sunfish and the water, and time ceased to exist as he ran before the wind. Here it didn't matter that he couldn't remember the past too clearly, or that the future was a minefield of lies and discovery.

Was this why you liked to sail? he wanted to ask Neil. *To escape from being a liar and a bully? To escape from yourself? Did you feel cleaner in the lake, in the wind? Did you feel safe?... So why did you go to the arcade that day when you knew you could come home and go out on the lake? Why did you go with Hank Miller?*

There was no answer as the far side of the lake rushed toward him. Reluctantly Cameron moved the tiller, tightening the mainsheet and ducking under the boom as the boat came about. He tacked upwind, avoiding Diana's hurt expression along with her bobbing boat, and came about for another run.

But this time the rushing air and the sense of surfing on top of the waves couldn't erase the worries. Cougar had said he'd find Cameron on Thursday, and that gave him less than two days to come up with some way to pay the man off. And Diana had made up her mind that he wasn't really Neil, just as Detective Simmons had.

He'd thought the Laceys had accepted him as Neil. He'd thought he might be part of a family at last. Now, faced with Cougar's threat and Diana's and Simmons's disbelief, and his own fear of what the lab evidence would disclose, even flying across the water couldn't wash out Cameron's fear that instead of being safe, he was cornered.

17

Threats

He got up his nerve to ask Diana if the Laceys had kept anything of Neil's. To his surprise, she told him right away that Stevie had been given most of the books and toys, and the clothes had been discarded as the years had passed and Neil would have outgrown them. But Diana said that her mother had saved the books and games and models that Neil had liked best; she just hadn't been sure he was ready for them yet. When she came home from the museum that afternoon, Cameron asked to see them.

His mother's eyes softened, and she reached to embrace him. He automatically warned himself not to flinch, but found himself leaning into her arms instead. She no longer squeezed him as tightly. Her arms felt secure, and he found he liked feeling them around him. He wondered if he had wanted her to hug him again, and if that was why he had waited for her to come home, instead of getting Diana to show him Neil's things.

She took him into the bedroom he'd been in only once before, when he'd asked his father about his punishment. The question of what was bothering him about the man's explanation still nagged at him, but he couldn't concentrate on it now. His mother was pulling a cardboard carton out of the closet.

"I hope we kept the right things," she said, sounding both worried and hopeful at the same time.

"I'm sure you did," he said uncertainly. She looked a little let down, as if she'd expected a different response, so he added, "I mean—it's been so long—I didn't think you'd still have anything."

"Of course we saved your things!" she said, shocked. "Oh, Neil—we always knew you'd come back to us. We wanted everything to be just the same for you." She looked away, embarrassed that so much was different. But Cameron knew it wasn't their fault things were different. It was Neil's, for going with Pop.

"It's just been too long," he said gently. "I'm glad you gave a lot of my stuff to Stevie when he was the right age for it."

She smiled at him and hugged him again. Then she stepped back, uncertainly. "I know—I hug you too much. You don't like it." She laughed a little. "Stevie doesn't like it, either."

Before he stopped to think, Cameron said, "I do like it, actually." He blushed, wishing he hadn't said anything. But it was the truth, however unexpected. He did like her arms around him, and he liked breathing in her flower scent as she held him.

This time her smile was tinged with tears. "You don't have to say that, Neil. It's just that it's been so many years for me, not being able to hug you."

Cameron leaned into her arms. "A lot of years for me, too," he told her. But he thought, *Too many years since the mother I can't remember—did she hug me? Did I like it or not? Could Neil's mother really love me in place of her son?*

Finally she released him. "There—take the box into your room. I know you want to look at your things by yourself."

He carried the carton away, leaving her sitting alone in the bedroom with a peaceful expression on her face.

In his own room, Cameron examined the stacks of age-softened baseball cards, the shoe box of too-bright dinosaur models, the jigsaw puzzle of John Paul Jones's ship grappling with the British warship *Serapis,* the worn copy of *Goldilocks and the Three Bears.* He paged through *Treasure Island,* with its large colored pictures, and *Ships at Sea,* with its one-page stories of great naval commanders throughout history and its pictures of tall ships firing on each other. But he found no clue as to what Neil had really been like. Had he been the selfish, spoiled bully Diana thought he was? Had he been a boy who pushed his mother away when she hugged him? Had he been someone whose return was worth waiting for all these years, or worth dreading?

More importantly, Cameron hadn't found anything he could use to pay off Cougar. He discovered that

Neil's parents had sentimentally kept a dormant bank account in Neil's name all these years. It had several thousand dollars in it toward a college fund, but Cameron knew they'd find out if he withdrew any, especially if he took out enough to keep Cougar quiet.

By Thursday morning he felt as trapped as if he'd been locked in the cellar all night. He'd lain awake far into the dark, trying to decide what to do. The Laceys weren't really rich, not like the boy's family who lived in the mansion. The Laceys had plenty of money, but it was in things, like the house and the boats and the cars. How could he pay Cougar what the man wanted?

And even if he paid off Cougar somehow, would he really be safe? For every moment of security, like the time with Neil's mother in the bedroom that day, and the time in the sailboat, he faced hours of suspicion from Diana and probably from Stevie as well. He'd seen the doubts flickering across his parents' faces, too. Did they really believe him, or were they just waiting for the evidence to come in? Evidence they hoped would set the doubts to rest, but evidence he knew would condemn him.

He had still been wide awake when Neil's father came in. The man paused at Stevie's bed but then came to stand at the foot of his own bed. Cameron breathed slowly and steadily, wondering whether the man really knew he was awake all along, wishing he could tell him about Cougar and ask for help. But Cameron didn't know how to ask anyone for help. He'd never done it.

Eventually the man walked quietly out of the room,

and Cameron slid into an uneasy dream-wracked sleep, haunted by Cougar's scarred face and heavy fist.

When he told Mrs. Pierson he was going to the library again that Thursday, Diana insisted on coming along.

"I remember the way now," he told her.

"Mom and Dad don't want you going off alone," she said virtuously. Since the argument last Thursday night, she hadn't said anything more in front of her parents about his not being Neil, and she made a point of calling him Neil when they were around anyone else. But he knew it was just acting. When they were alone, she didn't call him anything.

He took the nylon duffel bag that Neil's father had brought to the hospital, tossed in the library books he'd checked out with his new card, then strapped it to the carrier on the back of Stevie's bike. Also inside the bag was the jewelry he'd taken from his parents' bedroom.

Cameron hated himself for stealing it. He'd gone into their room Wednesday afternoon, when Stevie was out playing baseball and Diana was washing her hair and Mrs. Pierson was busy in the kitchen. He'd miserably opened the dresser drawers and gone through the carved mahogany jewelry chest and taken some things he hoped wouldn't be missed for a while. Holding the earrings and cuff links and necklaces had made him feel filthier than any of the things Pop had made him do. But he felt cornered and helpless, also, the way he always had when

Pop brought another boy home. And he felt angry—the way he had when he thought about how the grown-ups hadn't ever done anything to stop Pop. There was no one to stop Cougar but him.

After they parked the bikes and went inside the building, Cameron left Diana looking at videotapes and headed toward the children's room. When he was sure she wasn't watching, he doubled back and went outside the library. He left Stevie's bike in the stand, since she'd locked the two of them together with her chain again, and hurried on foot to the side street where Cougar had found him before.

The man was propped up in a doorway, waiting for him. There was a coarse black stubble on Cougar's pale cheeks and a haunted look in his eyes. He looked as if he hadn't changed his clothes since Monday. Cameron could almost see Pop shaking his head and thinking that if you stood out you got caught. Maybe the cops would pick Cougar up for vagrancy or something. But Cameron didn't know if that would help or just give Cougar the chance to tell the cops who Cameron really was.

"I knew I could count on you, partner," Cougar said, grinning at him. "What'd you bring?"

"I told you I couldn't get much," Cameron tried to warn him.

"Just give it here!"

Cameron fumbled with the zipper and pulled out the cloth-wrapped bundle of jewelry. Cougar spilled the pieces into his hand and poked them around with one dirty finger. "I can't live on this, brat! It's only a couple hundred dollars, maybe more if these pearls are real. What about cash?"

Cameron shook his head. "I told you—I can't get any."

"Blow it out the other side," Cougar said, smacking Cameron's head with a clenched fist. Cameron staggered a few steps, his ear ringing.

"Big house," Cougar went on, "boats, cars—there's money! You find it!"

"I can't!"

"You better." Cougar grabbed his T-shirt and pulled him so close that Cameron could smell that the man had been drinking. Cougar had always drunk more than Pop, and this was whiskey, not beer. Cameron remembered how vicious Cougar could be when he got drunk.

"No!" he cried, suddenly terrified. "Don't take me away!"

Cougar released him suddenly and laughed. "You? I don't want you! I want something I can sell to get some money. You're used goods."

Cameron felt as if Cougar had punched him in the stomach, even though this time the man hadn't laid a hand on him.

"I never get a break," Cougar mumbled, shaking his head. His voice turned whiny. "Always somebody else calling the shots. Even found a nice little mouse partner, like you, but I still can't get a break." He frowned. "Say—you got a key on you?"

Cameron shook his head numbly.

"Key to the house," Cougar said. "You get me the key, I'll get the money myself, or something I can sell easy."

"I can't," Cameron whispered, thinking in horror of Cougar going inside the Laceys' house.

"You get that key." The man's voice lost its bleary drunken lilt and sharpened. "I won't take you, but what about that pretty little boy the Laceys have—your pretend little brother? I could get real money for him in Knoxville."

"No!"

"You get me the key," Cougar ordered, "or little brother disappears."

15

Another One of the Boys

Diana found him sitting on the front steps of the library, hugging the empty duffel bag.

"What's with you?" she asked.

"I just wanted to get out," he said shortly, jumping up and leading the way to the bikes.

"Hey, you were the one who wanted to come, remember?"

Cameron nodded. "I know, but I'm selfish and moody and untrustworthy, remember? I guess I changed my mind."

She piled her books in her carrier basket and unlocked the chain. "Look," she said slowly, "I want you to level with me. I told you—I don't care who you really are, but I do care what you're doing to my family. Okay? I think you're in some kind of trouble and you're lying about it. Am I close?"

When he didn't answer she went on, "Well, I guess it's your business, but I want to know if your trouble is going to hurt my parents, or my brother."

Cameron climbed on his bike. Part of him wanted to trust her, but he'd never had a friend before. He'd never told anybody the truth about Pop back in Buckeye, and he hadn't told anybody now that he wasn't Neil Lacey. He hadn't even admitted anything to Cougar. If nobody knew the truth about you, nobody could see just how bad you really were.

"There's nothing to tell," he said, impatient to see Stevie, to make sure the boy was safe. "I just want to go home."

"Don't you want anybody to help you?" she demanded. "I told you—I don't care you're not Neil— I'm *glad* you're not. I like you, and I wish you really *were* my brother."

"I am," he said weakly.

"Come off it," she said. "Little things might change— okay, maybe Neil wouldn't remember the jokes he used to crack up over, maybe he'd even change what kind of books he liked reading. But what you're really like inside doesn't change, and you're not like Neil."

When he kept silent she folded her arms. "Okay. Then I'm going to talk to Dad tonight."

"No!" Cameron whirled on her. "You leave him out of this! And leave me out of whatever crazy story you're making up. I told you—I think you've always made things up. That's why your memories of me are so weird. And that's why you like acting, too, so you can act out your stories onstage. Well, leave me out of your pretend stories from now on!"

He stood up on the pedals and hit the street flying, not looking to see whether she was behind him. Cameron hated pushing her away when she wanted to help, but he couldn't let anybody get too close to him. She'd figured out too much already. And she was just a kid, like him. Even if he could trust her, she couldn't do anything about Cougar.

Diana caught up with him before they got to the lakefront road, and they coasted into the driveway together. But Cameron was off his bike and on his way down the back lawn before she could say anything, and that was fine with him. One lesson he'd learned early and well from Pop was that keeping quiet about things was always better than asking people for help.

He found Stevie down by the dock. The boy was wearing a life jacket and sitting half-asleep in the cockpit of the family boat, smiling as it rocked him gently. Cameron pulled on a life jacket and climbed in with him.

"Hey," he teased, "if you cross a lake with a leaky sailboat, what do you get?"

Stevie's eyes flew open, but he wouldn't play. "What do you want?" he demanded.

"Do you want me to take you out in the Sunfish?" Cameron asked, surprising himself.

"Why would you want to do that?" Stevie asked, suspicious.

Cameron shrugged. "I don't know. I just thought you might like it."

"You can't, anyway. Dad said I can't sail with anybody but him until I'm ten."

Cameron wondered why but didn't say anything. From what Diana had said, surely Neil used to sail alone, and he'd only been eight.

"Diana and me can't do anything on our own because of you," Stevie said angrily, as if he'd read Cameron's thoughts. "Mom and Dad think if they'd been stricter with you, you wouldn't have gone off. So they're taking it out on us."

Cameron looked at the water lapping against the fiberglass hull, urging the boat away from the dock, straining the mooring lines. "I'm sorry."

Stevie sighed. "You say that a lot now. You never used to."

"I've changed. Look, Stevie, I need to talk to you."

The suspicious look was back in Stevie's eyes. "About what?"

"I know you told me that you know not to go off with a strange man," Cameron began, feeling his way just like he'd ease the Sunfish into the wind. "But what about if somebody grabbed you?"

"What do you mean?"

"Suppose you were just walking along, say, and a car pulled up beside you and somebody opened the door and grabbed you and pulled you inside."

"Stop it!" Stevie shouted. "Nobody's going to do that!"

"Stevie," Cameron said, trying to be patient, "it happens. You know how you keep it from happening? You stay away from deserted streets. You don't walk close to the curb, and you never go near a strange car. And if a stranger comes up to you and tries to talk to you or tries to get you to go with him, you run away as fast as you can, and you shout for help. You find any grown-up you know, and you tell them what's happened, and they'll help you."

"Yeah, yeah," Stevie said. "Big deal. Nobody wants me, anyway, they only want you."

Cameron tightened his lips, thinking the boy didn't know how much someone did want him. "That's not true, Stevie. Look—you spend a lot of time alone, too much. I don't want you to go out alone—"

"*You* don't want?" Stevie yelled. "Who cares what you want? You're always off with Diana! You can't be bothered to spend any time with me, just like before. You don't care—so just let me do what I feel like, okay?"

"No, Stevie—" Cameron felt adrift. He thought of all the other boys who hadn't listened to him. Less than three weeks ago he'd tried to tell Josh to be good and do what Pop wanted, and Josh hadn't listened. *You're a chip off the old block*, Pop had always told him. *Only boy I ever found who knows what's good for him, and how to keep quiet about it—that's why I keep you around*. He'd tried to tell them, but none of them would listen. Somehow he had to make Stevie listen. "Look, this is important."

"*I'm* important!" Stevie retorted.

"Yes, you are!" Cameron yelled back. He stood up suddenly, towering over the smaller boy and rocking the boat wildly. "So you listen to me for once in your life! You never go off alone again, do you hear me? You stay with me or your sister all the time, okay? I promise to spend more time with you, and I'll ask Dad about taking you sailing, but don't go off alone!"

"I thought you'd changed," Stevie snapped back at him. "I thought you were nicer now, but you're just the same—bossy, telling everybody what to do. Today you want me to hang around you, next week you won't care! Well, I don't care—I'll do what I feel like!"

"Stevie—"

But the boy had already climbed out of the rocking boat and onto the dock, and was racing up the lawn toward the house.

Cameron climbed out of the boat himself and stripped off the life jacket, then stopped as he heard the sound of measured claps.

"Bravo," Diana said. She was sitting at the picnic table and had apparently watched the argument. "You're the actor—that was a great performance."

"Lay off," he told her.

"You're definitely not Neil," she said, grinning. "He'd remember how stubborn Stevie gets when you tell him something that sounds like an order. He'd always tell Stevie to do the opposite of what he wanted him to do, and then he got his way."

"Clever," Cameron said tiredly.

"He just knew Stevie. You don't."

She was right, he didn't know Stevie. But he liked the spunky little kid. Cameron didn't really know any of the Laceys, and yet he already liked all of them—no, more than liked. He loved them, and he wanted to be a real member of their family, not just an impostor. He wanted them to love him, Cameron Miller.

He sighed. But how could they love him? He wasn't their son. He was a fake—a counterfeit, who had stolen their trust and in return set Cougar loose to prey on them.

Cameron walked past Diana and went into the house. He went into their bedroom, but Stevie was nowhere to be seen. He had to stop Cougar from taking Stevie— from taking anything more from the Laceys, ever. But how?

16

Missing

He decided that for all her overdramatizing, Diana was right—it was time to talk to Neil's father. Cameron made up his mind to tell him about Cougar that night, but then his father called to say he'd be late for supper, and when he finally got in he looked tired and strained. Cameron had worked out his story, and he was torn between going ahead with it and not wanting to add to the man's problems.

During the late supper of lamb chops and tossed salad, Cameron eyed Neil's father, trying to make up his mind what to do. His plan was to say that Cougar had been a mean, dangerous man, and that he wanted revenge on Hank Miller because Hank had lied and that lie had sent him to prison. That much was easy, because it was true. And Cameron could say that he himself had lied, too, because Hank had told him to.

Because of that, Cougar had come looking for him and threatened to tell the police that he was Cameron Miller so they'd arrest him. And he would say that Cougar had frightened him so he took some jewelry to pay him off, but Cougar said it wasn't enough and now he wanted a key to the house so he could take what he wanted.

Cameron knew what the man had said before about punishment, but this time he might change his mind. Lying and stealing and putting the whole family in danger—this time there really might be a beating. But he didn't care. He knew he had been bad enough to deserve it. Besides, there was still that nagging feeling that something was wrong in what Neil's father had said last time. He loved Stevie and Diana, yet he had punished them by grounding them and ignoring them. What would he do to Neil if he believed he had done something truly bad? And Neil's mother had slapped Diana for only saying what she believed. Would she punish him even if his father didn't want to?

He couldn't follow that thought now. He had too many other things to worry about. He scraped the bottom of the bowl for the last of his ice cream for dessert, and waited for the others to finish, one knee jiggling impatiently under the table. Regardless of the punishment, when he told them that Cougar had threatened both him and Stevie, his father would get the police after the man. And maybe it wouldn't matter what Cougar said about his identity. The police already believed he wasn't Neil anyway, but his father was convinced he was. Cougar probably couldn't change the man's mind. Cameron hoped. Unless he really *had* been too bad.

He saw Diana studying him as he propped his chin on one hand, wishing Stevie would hurry up with his ice cream before it all melted into slush in his bowl. Diana had her head cocked to one side, and she was frowning slightly. He figured she was probably noticing more ways he was slipping up—probably Neil never sat like that. She was assembling his mistakes like puzzle pieces to form a pattern that would prove he wasn't her brother. He must be like one of those puzzles with no picture on the box, so you're trying to figure out what the picture must be as you put it together. When would she have enough pieces assembled to show her parents the distorted picture of a fraud? He couldn't stop to think about that now.

Finally Stevie slurped up the last of his ice cream. His father went into the living room with the newspaper and sat staring at the room's reflection in the darkened plate-glass window, the paper still folded on his lap and his briefcase open beside his chair.

"Bad day?" Cameron asked, following him.

"Hmm?" His father turned away from the empty window and half smiled. "A long deposition in a tricky case, that's all." He rubbed the side of his face and yawned. Cameron realized that all the fuss since he'd turned up in the Buckeye police station (had it only been two weeks?) must have been a problem for his parents at their jobs. He hoped neither of them would get into trouble because of him.

"Uh, Dad," he said, uncertain how to begin a conversation like this. He'd never tried to get Pop's attention about anything. He'd just as soon Pop ignored him in the evenings.

His father blinked and looked at him more closely. "Hey, what's that bruise on your face?"

Cameron ducked his head quickly. "I, ah, just fell off Stevie's bike," he said without thinking, then cursed himself for not simply saying Cougar had hit him. He was so used to lying about everything, it was hard to tell the truth.

"We've got to get you your own bike," his father said absently, believing the lie the way grown-ups always did. His mind seemed to be back on the difficult case. "We'll do that this weekend, okay? Oh, and I've set up our first family therapy session for next Monday. Don't worry"—and he smiled—"you won't have to go to it alone. We're a family, and we'll all do it together."

Next Monday seemed a lifetime away. Cameron wondered whether he'd be part of the Lacey family anymore by next Monday.

"Look, Neil, I need to look over some papers for tomorrow." Then the man focused on Cameron again. "Unless you need to talk to me about something?"

It was his chance to say he'd lied about the bruise and to tell the whole story about Cougar, but Cameron couldn't find a way to start. He swallowed and felt himself shaking his head. "Nothing special," he heard himself saying. "It'll keep."

He went out of the living room and headed to his

room, telling himself that waiting one more day wouldn't matter. Cougar wasn't going to do anything right away—he'd give Cameron time to get the key. Maybe he wouldn't be back until after the weekend. Wouldn't he assume that Neil's parents would be at the house all weekend? It would be a stupid time to break in. Cameron could tell his father tomorrow night, and the police could pick Cougar up on Saturday.

"Did you ask him?"

Cameron blinked back to the present and saw Stevie sitting propped up in bed in his pajamas, staring hopefully at him. In a flash he remembered promising to ask about taking Stevie sailing in the Sunfish.

"I tried to talk to him, Stevie," he said, which was true, even if it hadn't been about sailing. "But you saw him tonight—before I even got the question out he asked if it wouldn't keep. He said he had work to do."

"You didn't even bother to ask," Stevie said.

"I tried—"

"You're a liar," Stevie snapped. "He always had time for you."

Cameron's patience snapped. "Stevie, that was six years ago! You've blown it all out of proportion because I haven't been here! If I'd been here every one of those days I was missing, there'd have been plenty of times he wouldn't be bothered with me."

"You weren't here," Stevie said bitterly, "and every one of those days he did bother with you, anyway."

"Please, Stevie," Cameron said, wishing there were some way he could make up for all the years the boy had felt second-best to a ghost. "Look, let's do something else together tomorrow. You name it, okay?"

But Stevie threw himself down on his pillow and pulled the covers over his head and wouldn't answer. Cameron got slowly into bed and lay there, lonely, searching for the familiar ache he had felt for Pop. It was fading—more of an emptiness now than a real longing that Pop would return, with his rules and his belt and his love. But there was nothing to fill the emptiness. Cameron didn't dare fill it with Neil's father, knowing how disappointed the man would be in him when he learned the truth.

He wished desperately that he'd told him. *It's not too late*, he urged himself. *Get up and tell him it's important.* But he couldn't make his legs move. Never once, in all his confused memories, could he remember getting out of bed and going to Pop in the night. Never. He couldn't do it now.

Then he remembered that Neil's father would come to him. And maybe it would be easier to warn him about Cougar in the dark than it had been in the lighted living room, where everything seemed safe and orderly, and Cougar's threat would have sounded preposterous.

In his mind Cameron went over the story he planned to tell again and again, imagining Pop's narrowed eyes as he listened, judging the truth, deciding whether or not to use the belt. He went over it until he was sure it would convince even Pop, and by the time he heard the man's footsteps outside the door, he was confident he could explain the danger and be believed.

But when the man stopped at the foot of his bed, Cameron found himself unable to speak. *Don't make a sound,* Pop always told him, his whisper harsh in the dark. *Be good and everything will be all right. Don't make a sound.* And Cameron never had. He had never spoken in the dark. He'd thought he would be able to here, in this house where he was safely watched over in the night. But he couldn't break Pop's rule.

The man must have noticed something different about his breathing. He moved closer. "Neil?" His voice was low, so as not to wake Stevie. "Are you all right?"

Cameron heard a small sound escape from him, and went rigid with terror. *Don't make a sound.*

The man bent down and touched his shoulder. "It's okay," he said softly. "It's only a dream. Shhh." *Don't make a sound.* "Go back to sleep."

Heartsick, Cameron obeyed. He kept silent and slid into an uneasy sleep, knowing that the man was right. His time here, with this family, was nothing more than a dream. He wasn't good enough to deserve it for real, and he never would be.

Friday morning, he opened his eyes and escaped from the memory of blows and curses and the agonized screams of the other boys, as he huddled in the shadowy corner of a suffocating cellar, seeing Pop in his imagination walking toward each boy in turn with the handcuffs in one hand and the belt in the other. Exhausted, he looked over at Stevie's bed, but the boy wasn't there.

"Did he say where he was going?" Cameron asked Mrs. Pierson.

"He'll be around the house or the yard," she said, laughing. "There's a change, your asking about your little brother! But he's always off on his own, you know that."

Cameron cornered Diana in the family room, where she was watching music videos and reading a library book. "Have you seen Stevie this morning?"

"Hello to you, too," she said, and her voice sounded a little odd, almost uncertain for a change, and he wondered why. "What's the big interest in Stevie?"

"I felt bad about the argument yesterday, and I wanted to do something with him today to make up for it, that's all."

She shook her head in mock amazement. "Definitely not Neil." Her voice was back to normal now, so he guessed she must have just been caught up in her book. "But I mean it—I like you much better. Neil never felt bad about anything, and he never wanted to make up for anything, either."

Cameron felt a surge of anger. "Can't you forget about stuff I did six years ago and think about now? Have you seen Stevie or not?"

"Not," she said, shrugging and opening her book again. But her eyes stayed on him as he hurried out of the room.

He checked in the garage, but Stevie's bike was still there. Not that he'd necessarily use it, Cameron thought, since his big brother had taken it over, like everything else. He looked out in the road and saw a crowd of kids playing baseball, but when he jogged up to take a closer look he didn't see Stevie among them. He asked a couple of the kids, but they said Stevie hadn't come out to play that morning.

Where could the boy have gone? Cameron rubbed his ear where it still ached from Cougar's blow and wondered what he should do. Chances were that Stevie was just sulking, but what if Cameron had misjudged Cougar's threat? He'd thought Cougar would be careful and logical, like Pop, but he'd already realized how different the two men were. What if it had been a mistake not to tell his father last night, despite the case that had been worrying him? Could Cougar have taken Stevie already?

Cameron came back in the house to find Mrs. Pierson getting ready to leave for her shopping trip. Twice a week, Tuesday and Friday, she went to the grocery store. He assured her there wasn't anything special he wanted and watched her back her ancient Chevy sedan out of the driveway and thread her way carefully through the ball players, waving through her open window at them.

Cameron walked slowly through the house, thinking hard. If he could only find Stevie, he'd stick to the boy like glue until his father got home, and then Cameron could tell him and his father could handle it. But the fear of not knowing where Stevie was caught his chest in a vise and crushed him like the weight of Pop's body. He had to do something. Maybe Diana would tell him how to call the law office. Even if Cameron interrupted his father and got in trouble, and then Stevie sauntered in perfectly safe, it would be worth the explanations to have given the warning.

He went to the plate-glass window in the living room and stared at the lake, then scanned the lawn for any sign of Stevie. Suddenly Cameron looked back at the dock, and his eyes widened.

"Diana!"

He started for the side door and crashed into her coming out of the family room.

"What in the world—"

He interrupted her. "Call your father at the office, and your mother at the museum—get them here right away!"

"What's going—"

"Shut up and listen! Call Detective Simmons!" Cameron didn't care if she added his strange behavior to the list of things that weren't like Neil. It was too late for that. He'd tried so hard since he came to the Laceys', terrified that each mistake would be the one that gave him away, and it had all been a waste. He could have just enjoyed himself and not worried about how the mistakes were mounting up. Even if he had never slipped up once, he was blowing his cover for good now, and he would never be part of the Lacey family again. But his longing to belong wasn't as important as Stevie's safety. Cameron fished in his jeans pocket for the card the detective had given him on Monday. "Here, this number—call him and get him here, too." He already had the side door open.

"Why?" Diana shouted. "What do I tell them?"

"Tell them Stevie's in danger—look!" He grabbed her shoulder and pulled her out the door with him and pointed to the family's boat, at least a hundred feet away from the dock already, with the mainsail raised. "Stevie wouldn't ever cast off, would he?"

Diana shook her head, crushing the business card in her fist.

"I think Cougar—Bill Scott—has got him," Cameron said as he let go of her and raced down the steps.

"Why?" she screamed after him. Then, "Neil, be careful!"

"Because you were right," he shouted. "I've been lying to everybody—I'm not your brother Neil! I'm Cameron Miller. I sent Cougar to prison and now he wants to get even. He's taking Stevie!"

17

Payback

Cameron didn't waste time looking for a life jacket. It didn't matter how many rules he broke anymore, and he'd wasted too much time trying to explain things to Diana. He just hoped she'd keep her cool and make the phone calls. He wondered briefly why she'd called him Neil. And why bother to tell him to be careful? Probably she meant he should be careful with Stevie.

He slowed down enough not to tip over the Sunfish as he climbed inside, then slipped the mooring line loose and hauled up the sail. The sheet caught the breeze cleanly and billowed out, and he cast off.

He didn't think Cougar knew how to sail, and he doubted that Stevie would be much help to him. The jib was still down, and the mainsail seemed to be luffing instead of carrying the boat forward with any speed. The bow was turned nearly into the wind, Cameron realized, and Cougar didn't seem to know how to tack to keep moving.

Cameron maneuvered the lighter Sunfish up the lake and prayed that he was wrong. If only he could come up on the boat and find a frightened Stevie alone in it. Perhaps Stevie had tried to sail the big boat without knowing how, all on his own, just to get even with Neil for letting him down. But Cameron didn't believe in the prayer. And as he neared the boat, he saw he was right.

"Ahoy!" Cougar's voice floated down to him, thick and dangerously drunk. "Bring me the key, did you? Too late—saw the boy and decided to go ahead and take him. Get out on the far side of the lake, then bus down to Knoxville. Boy's worth more than a key, I figure."

"Let him go," Cameron called. "Take me instead."

Cougar laughed. "You're no good, I told you! You're used goods. But him—he's fresh chicken—pretty and young. I was like that once, you know." His face darkened.

Cameron was close enough to see Stevie's body hunched on one side of the cockpit. The boy looked dazed.

"Go on back!" Cougar was saying. "Family can have you instead!"

Cameron thought of all the other boys who'd died. He'd tried to tell them to be quiet and to do what Pop said. After, while they'd buried the boys, Pop always told Cameron it was their own fault. They'd run off, they'd wanted him to take care of them, then they'd refused to do what he told them to do. They were bad, even worse than he was. Cameron had tried to show them how to be good, but he should have done more. He had never tried to save one of them, never tried to help even one escape.

He'd known what Pop was doing to them; sometimes Pop even brought him up from the cellar and he saw for himself what happened. Even though he blanked it out, glimpses lived in the back of his mind and erupted in dreams he would wake from, silent and dry-eyed and rigid with terror. Yet he never told any of the teachers at school, never dared to try to tell the police. It wasn't right to blame the grown-ups because they should have known. It wasn't right to blame the boys for being so bad. He could only blame himself—he was as responsible for the boys' deaths as Pop or Cougar had been.

He didn't ask himself why he'd let Pop terrorize the boys. He didn't ask himself what he hoped to gain now. Cougar would probably kill them both—but not without a fight. Cameron let the wind fill his sail and aimed the Sunfish dead on at the boat where Cougar held Stevie. When he'd sat in the cellar dreaming of being out on the water, sailing had only been an escape for him. But he knew it could be a way to fight back as well as a way to escape. He remembered someone—it must have been one of the boys—a long time ago, telling him a story about John Paul Jones sailing at a British warship in a tight battle. He had closed with the British ship and grappled with it and finally boarded it. Jones had shouted something, too, something brave, but Cameron couldn't remember what.

The Sunfish closed on the larger boat and Cameron pulled in the sail until he felt like he was flying. *Ramming speed*, he thought, and then he hauled on the rudder at the last second and the Sunfish's bow crashed into the other boat's hull, skidded across it with a sickening scrape, and the two boats slammed together as he swung alongside in a jetting spray of displaced water.

"What the—" Cougar cried, but the impact flung him back against the far railing of the cockpit, and Cameron leaped onto the battered side of the Sunfish. It tipped wildly against the larger boat, and Cameron clung to the other boat's railing, ignoring the water splashing his already drenched legs.

"Stevie!" he cried. "Come on! Climb out."

But the boy only shivered, his eyes groggy, and Cameron realized he'd have to climb in and get him. Without warning, Cougar staggered up and brought a fist down hard on Cameron's right hand as it clutched the railing, but Cameron grabbed with his left hand and caught the man's wrist. He hung on it with all his weight, hoping to pull him overboard, but Cougar stumbled backward, lifting Cameron off the bobbing Sunfish instead. Cameron took advantage of the lift to throw his leg over the railing and grab on with his other hand.

Cougar struck him hard in the face with his left hand, and Cameron's eyes blurred dizzily for a moment, but he kept his grip and managed to topple over the side into the cockpit of the boat. Stevie trembled as Cameron's weight splashed the water on the deck onto him.

"Get rid of you for good," Cougar was saying. "Hank was crazy, keeping you alive all those years."

If he could throw the man overboard, that would be best, Cameron thought. He doubted Cougar could manage the damaged Sunfish, but Cameron could get Stevie safely back to shore, even if he wasn't really sure how to sail the larger boat properly himself. Cameron ducked as Cougar swung at him again. Then he slammed his body into the man's stomach, crashing him sickeningly against the cockpit railing.

Cougar gasped, his face turning gray.

Cameron grabbed the tiller and turned it, easing the boat out of irons so the sail caught the wind again. Cougar grabbed his hair from behind and jerked him backward. The tiller swung free, and Cameron slid in the water sloshing on the deck and cracked his head against the open hatch. Dazed, he tried to sit up as Cougar grabbed a handful of wet T-shirt and pulled him to his feet so that he could slug him first in his face, then in his stomach.

"How do you like that, you little prick?" the man snapped.

"Stop it! You leave him alone!"

Cougar seemed to sway and almost lose his balance at the sound of Stevie's shrill voice, and Cameron could see the boy grabbing at the back of the man's trouser leg. He looked around wildly for some weapon, but the boat was neat and bare. What weapon could there be in a sailboat, anyway?

Cameron thought of the Sunfish and wished he could

get at the daggerboard to use as a club. He wondered briefly about this boat, then realized that the center-board would be built in, to angle up on a block. He shook his head, trying to clear his eyes, and saw Cougar raise an arm to crash down on Stevie. He threw himself on the man and caught the arm, turning its force so it struck him instead in the chest.

"Stevie," he gasped, "the cabin—get in, and bolt the hatch!"

Cougar shoved him away and reached for Stevie as the boy tried to crawl toward the hatch. Cameron jerked the tiller again and once more the sail filled with wind as the boat swung violently about.

As Cougar struggled for balance in the rocking boat, he grabbed at Cameron's head again and missed, catch-ing only a handful of T-shirt from his back. He dragged Cameron toward him, jerking the T-shirt up and almost over his head so that it dug into his armpits, forcing his arms helplessly up in the air.

"Neil!" Stevie cried.

Cameron fumbled at the tangle of wet cotton and tried to pull his arms down to make sure the boy was all right.

"Your back!"

Shame burned through Cameron as he realized Cougar had pulled up the shirt far enough that Stevie could see the scars he'd tried to keep hidden. Then he told himself it didn't matter. After today he'd be gone from the Laceys, one way or another, and it didn't mat-ter what they thought of him. Cameron straightened his arms above his head and threw his weight backward, sliding out of the shirt and leaving Cougar tottering against the cockpit rail, clutching a handful of wet cloth.

"It's okay, Stevie," he said. "Just get in the cabin, now!"

But Cougar was already coming for them. Unlike Cameron, he'd been able to come up with a weapon. He'd unbuckled the thick leather belt he was wearing on his black jeans and was doubling the tongue over in his hand so that the heavy bronze belt buckle swung at the end of it.

Cameron crouched on the deck, staring at the belt, paralyzed with memories, until Stevie's scream of panic sounded shrilly behind him. He opened his mouth to say, *Just keep quiet,* and then cried instead, "No! Not this time!"

Then his voice gained strength and he heard himself shout, "I have not yet begun to fight!" He didn't know where the words had come from, but he felt their power surge through him.

The first blow of the belt wrapped the leather around his left arm until the buckle clawed into his biceps. Then, as Cougar pulled it back for another blow, Cameron rolled backward, knocking Stevie down the two steps into the cabin as the boat rocked dangerously. *There should be a door just beside the hatch,* Cameron found himself thinking as the belt whistled through the air again. The leather brushed past his side, but the buckle cracked harmlessly against the wooden hatch and Cougar swore.

There was no reason to believe that any door existed outside his imagination, but Cameron felt absolutely that his instinct was correct. He knew a door would be there.

And then he saw it. It was a small door, to the left side of the hatch. It had a little hook to fasten it closed, and it seemed to take his hand a long time to reach for the hook while the belt rose again in Cougar's fist.

The hook popped up and Cameron opened the little door and groped inside. His fingers closed around a cylinder, and he hauled it out, rolling toward Cougar to throw the man's aim off. He looked and saw that he was clutching a red fire extinguisher. Cameron fumbled with the nozzle, and suddenly foam spurted out, up into Cougar's face, and the man dropped his belt and began to scream, clawing at his eyes.

Cameron rose unsteadily to his feet and looked at the man warily. He remembered how Pop had struck him when he'd wanted to lame him instead of tie him, and the sickening pain that had left him helpless and immobile. Just to be sure he had time to get Stevie back safely, Cameron hefted the fire extinguisher in both hands like a baseball bat, and swung it with all the strength he had in his arms and his back and his legs, as though he were hitting a record home run, and struck Cougar a crippling blow on the big muscle in the man's thigh.

18

Not Neil Lacey

"Neil?"

Cameron turned his head to see Stevie beside him. He wondered how long he'd been standing there over Cougar's writhing body, the fire extinguisher swaying gently in his hand as the boat rocked. How long had it been since he'd first seen the boat heading away from the dock? It felt like hours.

"Are you okay?" Stevie asked.

Cameron smiled faintly at the boy. Neil's brother was a nice little kid, he thought. "Yeah," he said. "What about you?"

"My head hurts," Stevie said, rubbing it tenderly. "But I'm okay. Can we go home now?"

"Sure," Cameron said, and stepped over Cougar to turn the tiller.

"Here," he told Stevie, "hold the tiller like this until I tell you to straighten it out. I'll get the mainsheet."

They came about smoothly, and Cameron told Stevie how to angle the tiller so they could limp back at a fair speed even without the jib.

"What about your Sunfish?" Stevie asked.

Cameron looked at the damaged boat, but his mind had no more energy for solutions. "Leave it for now," he said finally. "Your dad can come back for it."

"Dad's at work," Stevie said.

Cameron sighed. "I hope not. Diana was supposed to call him and your mom. I told her to tell them you were in danger."

Stevie looked at him. "So were you."

Cameron shook his head. "That didn't matter."

Stevie looked like he didn't believe him, but he changed the subject. "Does your back hurt?"

Cameron turned away. Cougar was still moaning on the wet deck, clutching his thigh. He wasn't going anywhere. "No," Cameron told Stevie. "He got my arm pretty bad, and my head, but not my back."

"I mean, from before?"

"No," Cameron said shortly, cursing the boy's persistence. He just wanted to be quiet and feel the air in his face and the freedom of sailing one last time before Detective Simmons took him away and locked him up. But he guessed he couldn't blame Stevie for his curiosity.

"They're just marks, Stevie," he said finally. "They hurt then, but they don't hurt so much anymore." Cameron was surprised how true the words were. Why had he tried so hard to hide the scars? He finally added, "I just don't like thinking about them."

"Look!" Stevie shouted joyfully, jumping up from his seat at the tiller. "There's Dad in the yard! He did come!"

Good, thought Cameron tiredly, because he didn't know how to dock the larger boat.

"Stevie?" The man's voice sounded strained as he called from the shore. "Are you okay, Stevie?"

"I'm fine," Stevie cried, and burst into tears.

Strangely, the tears didn't make Cameron angry with the boy. Instead, he crouched down beside him. "Hey, Stevie, hold on a couple more minutes, okay? I don't know how to dock this thing, and I really need your help—can you help me?"

To his relief, Stevie sniffled, then rubbed his eyes and stood up straighter. "What do I do?"

Cameron looked out to shore. "How do we dock?" he called, afraid of meeting Neil's father's eyes.

"Neil?" There was a catch in the man's voice, but he'd called him Neil. Hadn't Diana told him the truth? "Are you hurt?"

"I'm okay," Cameron called, relaxing the sail to slow down. "But I don't know how to dock. And I wrecked the Sunfish. I'm sorry." And he *was* sorry, about everything. But that wouldn't make the punishment any less. Being sorry was never enough.

"Don't worry about it," the man called, his voice calmer now. "Just aim for the dock, drop the mainsheet, and watch out for the boom."

Cameron glanced down briefly to check Cougar, but the man still huddled on the deck of the boat, tears trickling across his unshaven face, catching in the puckered scar. Cameron looked away quickly, before tears could blur his own eyes, and showed Stevie how to aim. Then he dropped the sail and caught the boom as it swung back suddenly. He told Stevie to turn the tiller a little to the left so they'd come up beside the dock instead of crashing into it, then grabbed the mooring lines, and as soon as he thought Neil's father was in reach, Cameron threw first one line, then the second to him.

"We did it," Stevie said, delighted.

"Good sailing," Cameron told him.

His father was already lifting Stevie out as though he were a much smaller boy, and wrapping his arms around him, unmindful of the water from the boy's damp clothes spreading to his suit. Cameron felt relieved that Stevie was safe, but he wasn't looking forward to what was coming. His head and arm hurt, and he was so tired. He couldn't remember ever having felt so tired before, even after helping Pop bury one of the boys.

"Neil?"

He looked up slowly, and Neil's father held out one hand, still holding Stevie in his other arm. "Come on," he said gently.

Cameron took the hand and climbed unsteadily out of the boat, shivering from the cold water still sloshing across the deck. The broken bone in his leg that had healed badly gave way under him, so that he stumbled forward. Another hand caught him, and Cameron looked up to see Detective Simmons. He flinched instinctively, but the man's face didn't look as hard as he remembered.

Simmons said, "So you actually caught Bill Scott red-handed?"

Cameron pointed to the boat deck. A mess of foam and water had sloshed over Cougar's face as they docked, and he now lay groaning weakly.

"Neil? Stevie?"

The voice came from the side of the house, and Cameron realized that he hadn't looked around to see who was there. Neil's mother was running down the lawn, with Diana beside her. She must have just arrived.

"What happened?"

"I was just sitting in the boat, honest," Stevie explained, as his father passed him to his mother to hold. "I had my life jacket on and everything, just like you said, Dad. And that man came down to the dock. I heard the footsteps, but I thought it was Neil, because he'd said he wanted to do something with me today."

Of course, Cameron thought numbly. Stevie had been angry and hurt, but he hadn't gone too far away because deep inside he hoped his big brother would come find him and do something with him like he'd promised. Hope dies hard.

"But it wasn't Neil; it was this strange man. He smelled funny. And he climbed right into the boat, and when I asked who he was he said he was a friend of my brother's, and then when I told him not to untie the ropes he hit me."

Cameron winced, and sensed they were all looking at him.

"But then Neil came and got me," Stevie went on. "He sailed right up and smashed into the boat just like a navy warship—*POW!* He told the man to let me go and take him instead, and when the man laughed at him and called him something, I forget—used something—Neil climbed right up and fought with him! He made me get in the cabin, and the man hit him with his belt and there was this screaming and then everything got quiet, and when I came out the man was lying on the deck and there was foam everywhere and Neil said he'd take me home."

There was silence, and Cameron wondered how they were going to explain to Stevie that he didn't have a brother anymore, after all.

"Neil saved me," Stevie said, in case they hadn't got the point.

"He certainly did," said his father.

"I'm sorry," Cameron whispered. He stared down at the blades of grass and blinked his eyes. "He blamed me and Pop—Hank Miller—for sending him to prison, and he wanted to get even. He found out I was here and he came asking me for money." He shook his head. "I—I stole some of your jewelry to try to make him go away, but then he wanted the key to the house so he could look the place over himself and take what he wanted, and when I wouldn't he said he'd take Stevie."

He heard Neil's mother cry out, whether in anger at his taking her jewelry, or in horror at the danger he'd put Stevie in, he didn't know. He swallowed. "I tried to warn Stevie," he said, his voice so low that he didn't think anybody heard him.

"You tried to tell me last night, didn't you?" Neil's father asked suddenly.

Cameron nodded. "But I should have tried harder." His voice rose uncontrollably. "I should have tried harder to warn Stevie. I should have tried harder with all the boys—it was all my fault because I never tried hard enough!"

"Neil—" the man began.

"And I'm not Neil!" he shouted. "Didn't Diana tell you? I'm Cameron Miller! My father murdered Neil!"

19

The Last Body

There was a high-pitched scream, and Cameron looked up to see Neil's mother cover her mouth, squeezing Stevie tightly to her. *She'll hit me now,* he thought, *the way she hit Diana when she said I wasn't Neil.* But the woman just stood there, and this time Neil's father didn't go to her. He stayed close to Cameron.

"Neil—"

"I picked Neil Lacey from the files," Cameron interrupted. "Ask Detective Simmons—he can tell you about the files."

Simmons cleared his throat. He had handcuffed Bill Scott and was standing in the boat, holding the fire extinguisher in one hand. "Miller kept a file cabinet near where he buried the bodies, Mr. Lacey," he told Neil's father. "There was a file for every boy he had abducted and killed, a collection of news clippings about the missing boy and the search for him."

Neil's mother gasped, but his father was stony faced. "Go on."

Simmons sighed. "It's fairly common for serial killers to keep souvenirs of their victims. Sometimes they keep personal items, a watch, say, or a wallet, or photographs of each victim. Sometimes they'll keep locks of hair or something like that. Miller kept news clippings."

"And I read them," Cameron broke in. "I read them all. He'd lock me in the cellar while he did it, while he hurt the boys and then killed them, and I found the file cabinet because I was trying to get away from the smell, and I picked Neil from the files because..." His voice began to run down. "Because of the sailboats," he finished lamely. He shook his head and repeated uselessly, "I'm sorry."

"No!" Neil's mother said suddenly. "No—I don't believe it. This is—"

"It will be all right, Annie," Neil's father said quickly, glancing over to where she knelt on the grass, hugging Stevie. "Don't— Remember what the doctor said about the amnesia. Just wait. We have to get through this, but it will be all right. Trust me."

"But he lied to us—" Neil's mother broke off and she looked at Cameron with helpless bewilderment.

"Neil didn't lie," Stevie said, looking confused.

"He lied," Neil's mother whispered. She looked at Detective Simmons. "You were right," she said unsteadily. "You said you didn't believe in happy endings."

The detective cleared his throat again. "Mrs. Lacey," he said awkwardly, "I didn't buy that business about the amnesia at first. It just seemed too convenient. That's why I was so sure that Miller's son was taking advantage of you. And I have to admit—I was pretty angry with you, all of you—obstructing the tests." His eyes flickered to Neil's father's face. "Refusing to allow the DNA test."

Neil's mother looked uncertainly at her husband over Stevie's head, her eyebrows drawn together. "Jon?"

"I—" For once, the man seemed at a loss for words. "I was afraid," he said finally, his voice low. "Facts—every day I see how they don't always fit together to show the truth. I trusted what I believed—"

"But you thought he was lying!" she said, her eyes wide and shocked.

"No, Mrs. Lacey," Detective Simmons said quickly. "*I* was the one who thought he was lying, and I was wrong. I did a lot of work on my own time, some of it talking to guys on the task force—there aren't that many cases of kids surviving, but in nearly all of them the victims experience partial or complete amnesia. I guess it's the only way a kid can live with what's happened to him."

Cameron crouched on the lawn, shivering. What difference did the amnesia make?

Simmons went on, "And the tests—"

"Forget the tests," Neil's father said sharply. He came toward Cameron, and the boy recoiled. Now the punishment would come. If only he could remember the problem with what the man had said before, he might know what to expect. It was easier to bear if you knew.

"Please—I'm sorry I took the jewelry—I never

wanted to take anything. I didn't really pick Neil because of the money, even though Cougar said I did—it was the sailboats. I used to dream of sailing, when I was locked in the cellar, and while he—" He bit off the words.

Neil's father took off his suit jacket and knelt down beside Cameron. "Here," he said quietly. "Put this on."

When Cameron made no move to take it, the man draped it gently around his shoulders. Then he stood up and went back to Detective Simmons and took the fire extinguisher from him. He stood a moment, turning it over in his hands.

"How did you know where to find this?" he asked.

Cameron looked at him, confused. "I didn't. He was coming at me with his belt, and I didn't have anything. I kept thinking there must be something I could use somewhere, if I only knew where to look." He laughed shortly. "Neil would have known, you see? Neil would have remembered."

Cameron looked around until he saw Diana. She was standing near her mother and brother, her brown eyes dry, and almost kind. "Didn't you tell them?" he demanded. "She figured it out—she saw I wasn't like Neil, she saw I didn't remember Neil's jokes, or like the same kind of books, or know how to talk to Stevie, or anything."

"I saw you were a lot nicer," Diana said softly. "But last night, and today—the way you fidgeted in the dining room, and the way you rushed around, so determined to find Stevie—it was like you weren't trying so hard, and you seemed more like Neil would be..." Her voice trailed off.

Cameron remembered how worried he'd been about Cougar. The part of his mind that rigorously kept track of Pop's rules and made him watch his every move had been focused on keeping Stevie safe, so he guessed he must have been acting more on instinct. But Diana wasn't making any sense—his instincts should have made him act less like Neil than ever, not more.

After a moment, Neil's father asked, "How did you find the fire extinguisher, then?"

"I don't know—I was looking for anything, for a door, for something—and I saw this little door with a hook on it, and I unhooked the latch and reached inside, thinking there might be something I could use."

"And you found this?"

Cameron glanced at the fire extinguisher, wondering what difference all this made, and nodded.

"So you used it?"

He nodded again. "I—I shot it in his eyes, and he screamed like it hurt a lot." He winced again. "I'm sorry. I just wanted to make him stop."

"I hope you blinded him," Neil's father said flatly. "Don't waste another thought on him. What did you do next?"

Cameron frowned. "I was afraid he'd wipe the foam out of his eyes and come for me or Stevie again, so I hit him in the leg. Hank—Pop hit the boys on the thigh so they couldn't run. Me, too, when he got mad." He saw Neil's father brace himself as though against a blow, and felt the guilt and shame burning up into his face. He made himself go on. "Then Stevie came out of the cabin, and we sailed back. I'm sorry about the Sunfish. Will it be all right?"

"It'll be fine," the man said, taking a deep breath. "Now, why did you open that compartment?"

Cameron shrugged. "It was the only door I saw."

"There are compartments all around the sides of the cockpit, for storing extra sails and sheets and gear. Why did you open that one?"

"What difference does it make?" Cameron asked tiredly. Why didn't Detective Simmons just put another pair of handcuffs on him, and take him away with Cougar? "It must have been the first one I saw."

"I don't think so," Neil's father said. "I think you went for that one because you knew what was in it."

"But—" Cameron looked at him blankly. "How could I have known? I've never been on board that boat before."

"Neil has."

"But—"

"That was Neil's special hiding place," his father went on, in that dispassionate voice. "He put things there for safekeeping whenever we went sailing. The last thing he insisted on putting there was this fire extinguisher. Even though it was a pretty crazy place to put it from an adult's perspective, I could see it was an easy-to-get-to place for a little kid. And after he disappeared, I left it there."

"But I couldn't know that," Cameron said.

"Neil knew it."

"But I'm not Neil," Cameron whispered.

Neil's father walked over to him and sat down directly in front of him, oblivious to the damp grass. "Listen to me. The head of the forensics team phoned me this morning, before Diana called. They've been working overtime to identify the bodies, to set the other parents' minds at rest. I guess they used the files you saw as an aid to match the dental records and other features with specific boys from the missing children list, and they have identified every body but one. That one is not Neil."

"But there were twenty-two files," Cameron said unsteadily. "And you said there were twenty-three bodies. One was the new boy, Josh, so the others had to match the files."

"Yes, twenty-one of them did. The one that didn't match was a young boy, probably six or seven."

"No." Cameron shook his head. The man wanted his son back, he could understand that. But Cameron couldn't go on living somebody else's life. He had to make him see the truth. "He was short, the file said Neil was short. A short eight-year-old might look six, but—"

"It doesn't matter about his height," Neil's father said evenly. "That's not how forensics determines age from bones. That body wasn't Neil. For a start, the dental records don't match, even remotely. That boy had cavities Neil never had."

Cameron looked at him, confused.

"You're Neil."

He shook his head. "I'm Hank Miller's son. He told me I was his son. I'm Cameron."

"He lied. The last body is Cameron Miller."

Detective Simmons said, "Neil, the lab found clear evidence that the boy was related to Miller." He paused, then went on, "Miller beat the boy so hard that his bones had been broken and mended and broken again."

Cameron felt a shudder deep inside his chest, remembering his own broken bones, and how Pop had backed off the times he'd realized how badly he'd hurt him. Even being careful, Pop had broken bones sometimes, and blamed Cameron for it even as he set them.

He forced himself to keep motionless. He could hear the screams of the other boys still ringing in his ears, nearly drowning out the detective's voice. Of course, Pop hadn't had to be careful of them.

"Forensics could tell from the body that this boy had been battered from babyhood," Simmons was saying. "Then Miller killed him. But enough people knew that Cameron existed that he needed to find someone to take his place."

Neil's father took a deep breath. "Do you want to know what I think happened? How I'd explain this to a jury? I think Miller probably killed his son by accident, while he was beating him, but it made him realize that he liked the killing even more than the beating, so he began looking for boys. He took you. I think he intended to kill you, except that you were too good a survivor. So he decided that you should become his son and stop any questions about Cameron's disappearance. But he liked the killing, too, so he took other boys and killed them. Does that ring true?"

Cameron swallowed. "He said I was the only boy he'd ever found who knew what was good for him, and how to keep quiet..." He could barely hear his own voice repeating Pop's words.

"Listen to yourself," Neil's father urged. "'The only boy he'd ever *found*.' You weren't his son. You're Neil. You're *my* son. And I think you chose us because you knew, deep down, that you were Neil, even though you weren't ready to remember it yet."

Cameron held the jacket around his shoulders, his fingers rubbing the light summer wool, straining to understand what hadn't rung true about that talk on punishment and love. He looked at Neil's father, and saw instead a hazy memory of a different man, wearing jeans and a black windbreaker, towering darkly above him. He remembered how his own fingers and palm, and even his wrist, had disappeared into the man's grasp when he gave him his hand and let the man lead him to the car. That man had been Pop.

"He said he had to punish me for misbehaving," Cameron said slowly, "for going off alone." There were so many times he had been punished that they blurred into a single memory, like a needle locked into a scratch on one of the old vinyl country music records Pop listened to. But one punishment had been different, hadn't it? There was one time, so far in the past that he wasn't completely sure if he'd lived it or dreamed it.

"He said I'd been bad." He had always been bad, but that time was worse. And it was what Pop had said that time that had made him try so hard afterward, not the beatings. "He said—if I was good, maybe I could go home. So I was good. I did what he said, and I kept quiet."

Go home? What was he saying? He'd been home. That couldn't have been the hope that had made him hang on. Cameron shook his head violently. "Hank Miller was my pop—I only *wanted* him not to be. I only wanted to sail…"

The man in shirtsleeves, not the huge man-shape in his memory, said, "Think about the sailing. You used sailing to escape because Neil loved sailing and got away from everything when he sailed." He smiled, his eyes oddly bright. "You think that little refresher course taught you how to sail my boat today? No beginner could have done that. That was memory, Neil's memory, from when I used to take him sailing."

Cameron turned away from the urgency, staring at the grass instead of at Neil's father. He remembered Pop bending over him just as urgently, shaking his head at him. Cameron remembered suddenly how hard it had been not to cry that time, although he'd thought he had already learned never to cry. "He said my parents didn't want me back, because I'd been too bad." Cameron's voice sounded rusty in his own ears. "He said I had to be punished, because of what I'd done. Until I could learn to be good, they never wanted to see me again."

"No!"

Cameron dimly heard a woman's voice, as though from a long way away, but he was locked in his memory, and he could still feel the pressure of Pop's arms around him, dangerous and reassuring at the same time. The words came slowly, as if he were drugged. "He said, even though I'd been so bad, I could stay with him and be his son. He said he'd teach me how to be good, because he loved me, even though it would be very hard to teach me because I was so bad. He said Neil didn't exist anymore, and there was only Cameron."

He stared at the grass in silence for a few moments, sensing the truth in his buried memory of Pop's words. This was the nagging thought he'd been chasing about punishment. He looked up into a different father's face. "When he beat me, he said you wanted me to be punished because I'd run away. But then you said you wouldn't punish me like that."

"He lied," his father said, his voice thick.

He looked at the sunlight sparkling on the little waves in the lake, and felt the light begin to dance in his heart. The beatings hadn't meant love. This man's firmness and quiet faith in him meant love. Hank Miller hadn't beaten him because he loved him. He'd beaten him because he loved the beatings. He'd beaten him to beat Neil out of him. The punishment had never been to help him be good enough to be forgiven so he could go home at last. He'd found his own way home.

"I was looking for a door," he said finally, remembering his inexplicable certainty that there should be a door nearby. It was as though the silent, frozen places inside him were splintering apart and memories were melting into his consciousness. "I knew there should be a fire extinguisher inside that compartment."

"Yes," his father said.

"But you thought he was lying," the woman cried, her voice trembling helplessly like the voices of the boys. "You wouldn't even allow the DNA test."

"Mrs. Lacey," Detective Simmons interrupted, "even though your husband wouldn't permit the test—" He cleared his throat. "We had samples from the hospital tests, and we obtained samples from Mr. Lacey's physician, and I—well, I ran the DNA test anyway. I trusted my instincts—they've always been right." He looked down. "Until now, anyway."

His father looked up sharply. "You law enforcement officers think you can just bend the law any way you choose because of your *instincts*! I should have you brought up on charges for violating our civil rights—" Then he broke off, and sighed. "But I suppose this time it's best to just let it pass. I already know the results."

Detective Simmons nodded, looking relieved.

Cameron—no, Neil stared up at the two men. After all his fear of the toeprints and the dental charts, the evidence had been on his side all along. "I've changed," he said finally. "I'm not like the Neil he took."

His father nodded again. "You're yourself. We all change as we grow."

He looked up and saw his mother, tears running down her cheeks. Suddenly he heard again that voice reading him the Goldilocks picture book, and the story about John Paul Jones from *Ships at Sea*—it had been a woman's voice, not a boy's. His mother's voice. *She* was the one who had read him Jones's ringing cry, "I have not yet begun to fight!" and given him the courage to stand up to Cougar—the real mother he hadn't been able to remember because Hank had said she didn't want him back until he could learn to be good.

He wanted to tell her, to thank her, to feel her hug him as she hugged Stevie, as she had hugged him only—yesterday? But she was looking at him as if he had turned into a stranger. He blinked back his own tears. Maybe happy endings didn't exist, after all.

He stood up stiffly, pulling his father's jacket around him, and looked at Cougar standing beside the detective. He turned to his father. "Cougar's father...hurt him like Hank hurt me," he said in a low voice. "I'm a lot like him, I think."

Beyond his father, he could see Diana, hands on her hips and head cocked to one side, smiling at him. She'd told him to be careful even when she suspected he wasn't her brother. And there was Stevie, looking up at him admiringly. He looked away, embarrassed.

"I don't know what kind of person I am," he made himself tell his father, making sure the man knew the worst. "I let all those boys die so I could save myself. I'm afraid of growing up like—him."

The man had said he could trust him from the beginning, and he smiled now, clear hazel eyes reflecting his own. "You won't," he said. "I promise you. You couldn't have saved those boys, but you saved Stevie. You're nothing like that man. You're my son."

The promise was more than he had hoped for, more

than he deserved. He looked back at his mother. She had read that story about John Paul Jones to him over and over, each time he'd asked. If she could give him the courage he'd needed to save Stevie, then surely her love would be strong enough to forgive him in time.

I'm Neil, he told himself, and felt the tentative beginnings of hope uncoil to fill the emptiness in his chest.

Elaine Marie Alphin graduated from Rice University in Houston, Texas, with a triple major in history, English, and political science. She has written numerous books for younger readers and more than two hundred articles for children's magazines. She lives in Madison, Indiana.

Visit her Web site at **www.elainemariealphin.com**